JAMES
THE CONNOISSEUR
CAT

Harriet Hahn

JAMES

THE CONNOISSEUR CAT

JAMES

THE CONNOISSEUR CAT

HARRIET HAHN

ST. MARTIN'S PRESS
NEW YORK

JAMES THE CONNOISSEUR CAT. Copyright © 1991 by Harriet Hahn. All rights reserved. Printed in the United States of America. No part of this book may be used or reproduced in any manner whatsoever without written permission except in the case of brief quotations embodied in critical articles or reviews. For information, address St. Martin's Press, 175 Fifth Avenue, New York, N.Y. 10010.

Design by Diane Stevenson • SNAP-HAUS GRAPHICS

Library of Congress Cataloging-in-Publication Data

Hahn, Harriet
    James the connoisseur cat / Harriet Hahn.
        p. cm.
    ISBN 0-312-06382-2
    1. Cats—Fiction. I. Title.
PS3558.A3235J36 1991
813'.54—dc20   91-21813
                                           CIP

First edition: October 1991

10 9 8 7 6 5 4 3 2 1

CHAPTER 1

I spend a lot of my time in England. My apartment in Baron's Chambers, on Ryder Street, is my headquarters.

This November morning I struggled with my suitcases, and standing on the pavement, I pushed the button marked Inquiries, gave my name, and was admitted. Inside was the familiar tiny space in front of the ancient elevator, whose filigreed brass outer cage gleamed; its car, of mahogany, pierced by four beveled-glass window inserts, was still polished to a high shine.

I felt wonderfully at home, and then I noticed something new. Sitting on the small table where one usually finds messages and brochures describing current exhibits and events sat what appeared at first glance to be a big, gray, short-haired cat. It was motionless and its eyes were closed, but even so, I felt the power of a rare personality.

I stopped with my hand on the elevator door and did not exactly stare, but acknowledged that I was in the presence of something unusual.

"How do you do?" I heard myself ask.

The cat, which looked as though it were made of silver with a florentine finish, barely opened its eyes, gave me a long look, nodded, and slithered off the table.

I opened the elevator door. The cat strode into the car, stood on one side as I hauled in my suitcases, jumped

1

on top of the largest one, and, after I had closed the doors safely, patted a gray paw on the button marked 6. Cat, luggage, and I rose slowly and with great dignity to the top floor. Mrs. March, who manages Baron's Chambers, was waiting for us. She is short, lively, of indeterminate age and great energy. She is enormously efficient, knows how to solve any domestic problem, and is meticulous in collecting her bills. We like and respect each other, having done business for some years. The sixth floor of Baron's Chambers is hers. Here she has her office and apartment. The cat preceded me out of the elevator. Mrs. March propped open its door so that no one could summon it with my luggage in it, and we retired to her office.

"Let me introduce you to James," she said as she handed me my keys.

The gray cat sat on the desk and looked me over. His eyes were golden and they glinted.

"He hasn't been here long," she went on as she entered information in her ledger. "He appeared at my sister's house a month or so ago, and since Sylvia—that's my sister—was going to Cyprus on holiday, she dumped him on me."

An expression that could only be called hopeless resignation seemed to cross James's face.

"In any case, I hope he will not be a nuisance. If he is, chuck him out and let me know."

"I am delighted to meet you," I found myself saying to James, before I thought about how silly it was to talk to a cat.

James gave me the ghost of a nod.

I thanked Mrs. March, signed what she needed

2

signed, and started for the elevator. James followed, slipped in as I closed the doors, and sat on my suitcases as we rode down to the fourth floor. We disembarked, James and I.

My flat faces a narrow street. It has a generous sitting room with sofa, easy chairs, a table, and proper chairs for seating four people for a meal, as well as a bedroom, a small kitchen, and a bath. It is old-fashioned, with high ceilings, charming chintz curtains at the tall bay windows that look out on the street, and in the corner of the sitting room is a big television set.

I opened the door, and James strode in. While I started to unpack, he inspected the apartment. Once he was satisfied that everything was in order, he sat on the bed and watched. Soon he was bored and began to disappear. At one moment he was sitting on one of the beds. I looked away to put underwear in a drawer, and when I turned around he was gone. I looked all over the room, and then all over the flat. No James. A little at a loss, I returned to the unpacking, and when I looked again, there was James, sitting on the bed, grinning.

"You're a wizard!" I said indulgently.

James nodded.

I finished unpacking by carrying a bottle of Laphroaig single-malt whiskey into the kitchen. I put the bottle on the counter, and was amazed to see James on the counter, wrapping himself around the bottle. His golden eyes were gleaming.

"You like Laphroaig?" I asked.

James bobbed himself up and down to indicate his enthusiastic acquiescence.

"Ice?"

James sneered.

"Water?"

James shook his head.

I poured a dollop of Laphroaig in a saucer for James, and a dollop in a tumbler with some water for me, and carried both into the sitting room. I put the saucer on the coffee table in front of the sofa. James sat on the table and took a sip. Then he sighed contentedly and gave me a grateful smile.

We drank in companionable silence. James hopped off the table and curled up beside me. I tentatively extended my hand and stroked the silver head. James began to purr. This was not an ordinary purr, but a great deep roar of contentment.

I got up, turned on the television for the news, and returned to the sofa. We watched the news alertly for a few minutes, and then both of us closed our eyes. It is easier to concentrate on the news if you are not distracted by the picture.

There was a knock at the door.

James was instantly awake. He streaked for the door and sat waiting for me to open it.

There stood Mrs. March.

"Sorry to disturb you," she said apologetically. "Have you seen James?"

I was about to answer when I looked past her to the stairway that embraces the elevator. There, on the stairs, sat a proud, imperious cat. He was looking at Mrs. March as though she were slightly defective.

"He's right there!"

4

"So he is!" Mrs. March turned and started upstairs. "Sorry to have bothered you."

"See you tomorrow, James," I called softly. James swished his tail and stalked off.

I closed the door and went back to the sitting room, feeling a curious sense of loss. Outside, the drizzle continued. Inside, it was warm and cozy, but I felt bereft without my new friend. Even though I was in my favorite London neighborhood, with Christopher Wren's St. James Church just up there, St. James's Palace comfortably over there, Fortnum & Mason's department store close at hand, fine art shops and antique dealers all around, and, up the street, Thwaite's auction house, known since 1740, where painting, sculpture, furniture, wines, stamps, coins, and in fact anything large or small that is rare, valuable, and in demand, can be—and constantly is—auctioned, somehow all the sparkle had gone out of the day. Lingering, however, was the awareness that a most unusual personality had entered my life. This year's trip to London would not be routine, I was sure of that.

The next morning I was slow in getting started. (I do general research and am an agent in the fine-art business. I inspect objects offered for auction and bid on them for clients, for which I earn a commission. I also do research for three or four academics who are writing learned books on various historical subjects. I am then listed in the preface of the book under "My profound thanks to . . ." For this I also get paid.) When I finally stood in the hall, locking my door, I heard voices downstairs, and peered down the elevator shaft. I could not make out the words at first, but at last I could hear a man's voice.

5

"Take the suite for a week, dump your suitcase, and bring me down the key," it said.

Then I heard a little shriek. "Look at that cat," squeaked a different voice. "Go 'way!"

I heard the elevator door open. Then it closed and the cat was wrapping himself around her legs. Suddenly the cat switched his attention from the girl to her suitcase and began to claw at the canvas bag.

The young woman began trying to hit the cat with her purse. She was frantic. "Get away!" she cried over and over again.

When the elevator reached the sixth floor, it immediately began to descend. No one had gotten out.

Slowing, pretending I was reading a catalog, I walked down the stairs that encircled the elevator shaft. Inside the cage, visible through the beveled-glass windows, was a girl on one side and a cat on the other.

I arrived near the bottom at the same time the elevator reached the ground floor.

Grabbing her bag, the girl opened the doors and leaped out.

James sat in the middle of the cage.

"What's the matter?" asked a man who was standing in the tiny lobby.

"We're not staying here!" said the girl. "I can't bear that cat. We will have to find some other place to hide the stuff."

The man made an attempt to persuade the young woman to return and rent an apartment.

James sat in the middle of the elevator and glowered.

Shortly the pair left.

6

"We didn't want them here, did we?" I said to James as I shut the door to the elevator so that someone else could use it.

James was back on his table. He shook his head.

"Come by about five-thirty?" I asked as I left.

James beamed and nodded.

I had a lot to think about as I headed for the Green Park tube station. There was some evidence that the man and woman were up to no good, but how had James known? Clearly he was no ordinary cat.

That afternoon, promptly at five-thirty, there came a scratch at my door, and there was James.

I welcomed him enthusiastically, and we settled down to have a drink and watch the news.

A great sense of contentment filled me as I sat with the big silver cat on my lap. I stroked his head, he purred with delight, and time slipped by.

Then, as usual, Mrs. March came for him, and James played his game on the stairs.

This became our routine. At the end of a week and a half I felt confident enough to move our relationship a step further.

As James, pleasantly full of whiskey, sat on my lap, I said, "You understand everything I say, don't you?"

James nodded somewhat sleepily.

"Have you ever been out of this building?"

James shook his head.

"Ever seen any other cats?"

James shook his head.

"Ever killed a mouse?"

James shuddered.

7

The television said, "We interrupt this program to bring you a special report from the Prime Minister."

James shifted on my lap and, with an imperious gesture, placed a gray paw on my mouth as I began to ask another question.

He then sat up, alert and interested, to listen to Margaret Thatcher. He is a staunch conservative.

So I summed up to myself. James knew no other buildings in London, hated mice, and had never seen another cat. Perhaps he needed some education.

The very next evening we had just settled down when my telephone rang.

A friend was calling to tell me of a reception at Thwaite's.

"James," I said, putting my hand over the receiver, "do you want to go to a party?"

He was immediately awake. His eyes gleamed, and he nodded enthusiastically.

I called Mrs. March and asked her if I could borrow James for the evening. She was agreeable as long as he was not a nuisance, and so, when I had changed my clothes and my umbrella, James and I set out down the street for Thwaite's. James walked close beside me and looked up and down and around the lighted street.

"James," I said as we walked along, "there may be a problem about getting you in. I have a friend who has an invitation for me, but no one would think of inviting a cat."

I should not have worried.

We arrived at the entrance to Thwaite's together, and suddenly James had disappeared. I met my friend and we

8

entered. Our invitations passed the security check, and we went up the wide staircase, past huge urns filled on this occasion with arrangements of Scotch pine branches and soft gold chrysanthemums, into the great room where important auctions were held, as well as receptions like this one.

The walls of the great room and the open area surrounding the entrance were filled with pictures, and under them were pieces of furniture waiting to be auctioned.

This reception was to promote the sale of the furniture and porcelain of the Earl of Haverstock, Henry Stepson. There was an unusual amount of interest in this sale, because Haverstock Hall had recently been the scene of a robbery, and the police, as far as anyone knew, were mystified. The house had been ransacked, and a collection of particularly valuable unset rubies and diamonds had been stolen from the safe in the library, in which Lord Henry's secretary had been tied up and locked in a closet.

There had been a good deal of newspaper space devoted to the robbery, and even some TV time, so many people who would otherwise have ignored Lord Haverstock or Haverstock Hall were flocking to see his things.

I picked up a glass of wine from a tray and wandered around looking at paintings of dogs and horses and French furniture, and chatting with the people at Thwaite's whom I had met in past visits.

"Look at this collection of porcelain cats," said William Boots, an old and respected antique dealer.

Boots was looking at an elaborately ornamented sideboard on whose marble top sat a gray porcelain cat with blue eyes; a matching blue bow was tied around its porcelain neck. Right next to this cat was a large gray cat, a real one, facing the porcelain one. This gray cat had no bow, but instead wore an expression of sickening affection. Both cats were motionless. I had found James. James had found a love object.

"Come now," I said hurriedly to Boots. "That cat's just junk, not worth the fifty-pound estimate in the catalog. Now, that ormolu clock over there is worth looking at."

As I moved Boots away, I hissed, "No!" in James's direction.

When I looked back a few minutes later, James had disappeared.

I went off to dinner with friends to gossip about Lord Henry and to speculate on what prices the auction would bring.

"What about the cat?" I asked during the evening. "There is a fine Staffordshire porcelain cat in next week's sale, and the rest of the material in this sale is reasonably good, but that cat is a piece of junk!"

"Lawrence Dobbs brought it in at the last moment," said a Thwaite's man. "He's Lord Henry's secretary, and we are including it as a favor to him, otherwise we would never handle it at all."

It would appear that James had fallen in love with a piece of junk. Perhaps, I thought, familiarity would breed contempt.

"You wouldn't have a picture of that cat?" I asked.

"Well, I have a picture of the sideboard, and it has the cat on it. Would that do?"

It would do nicely, and eventually I returned to

Baron's Chambers. James was pacing the hall in an agony of nervousness, waiting for me. His coat was scruffy and his expression painful. I let him into the flat and dropped the picture on the floor. James fell on it, rolled on it, lay on it, and began to purr.

"James," I said, "I promise to get that cat for you at the auction if it doesn't go over fifty pounds."

James leaped onto my lap, sneering.

"All right, I'll go to a hundred."

He shook his head vehemently.

"A hundred fifty, but no more," I said finally. Realizing that I had reached my limit, James agreed.

That night, James slept on the floor, on the photograph.

Someone knocked at about eleven-thirty that night, but I didn't answer. I suspected it was Mrs. March, and she would not have approved.

Next morning early there was a fateful knock. I opened the door to let James out to play his game, but he did not respond.

"He's been here all night!" exclaimed Mrs. March. "Come along now," she said sternly, and James meekly shuffled out of the apartment. His coat was ruffled, his head sunken, his eyes dull. Sick with love, he crept from the room. Mrs. March shooed him along.

On the floor of the living room was what was left of a photograph of a sideboard with a cat sitting on it, patted nearly to shreds.

"Don't worry," I called after him. "I'll get it."

He gave me a pathetic look and plodded upstairs.

That evening when I came home, James scratched at

11

the door and slunk in. I gave him a glossy color photograph of the cat, which I had taken myself at Thwaite's. He was disgusting. He lay on the floor and licked it.

"James," I said seriously. "You must realize that this is a china cat. It is not real. It is cold and unfeeling. It will bring you no affection. It will not even fight with you. It cannot."

James left his love and leaped onto my lap. He placed a paw firmly over my mouth. He did not want to listen to reason. What cat in love does?

I offered a sip of Laphroaig. He declined. He lay on the photograph on the floor and sighed.

"I'll get it for you tomorrow morning."

James curled up on the photograph and fell into the sleep of one exhausted by searing emotions.

I called Mrs. March and told her not to expect James until morning. She finally agreed it was all right.

I was at the auction room promptly at eleven the next morning. I had not seen James after he plodded out of the apartment at six-thirty, but as I sat down in the auction room I felt a furry back brush against my leg, and I knew he was there. The room was fairly full. The publicity over the robbery had done its work, and it seemed there would be a nice profit for all.

The first item to be sold was the porcelain cat. That was why I was on time.

"A fine porcelain cat," said the auctioneer in a lifeless voice. "Been in the Haverstock family for years, and was a favorite of the late Lady Matilda Haverstock. I shall open the bidding at fifty pounds."

I lifted my program to indicate I would accept the bid.

"I have fifty pounds. Do I hear sixty?" said the auctioneer.

There was a movement somewhere else.

"I have sixty pounds. Do I hear seventy?"

I felt a sharp scratch on my ankle, and dutifully raised my program.

"I have seventy pounds. Do I hear eighty?"

He heard eighty.

"I have eighty pounds. Do I hear ninety?"

James scratched and I raised my program, but it appeared that someone else was interested in this worthless porcelain cat, and on looking around, I saw that it was Lawrence Dobbs. He looked nervous.

The bidding continued.

"I have one hundred fifty pounds. Do I hear one hundred sixty?"

It was up to me, and I had gone to my limit. James scratched fiercely, but I ignored him. Once he knew he'd lost, he disappeared.

"Going once." The auctioneer looked hopefully at me. "Going twice, and all gone." The cat was sold, and at a much better price than anyone would have imagined. The auctioneer's assistant held the cat aloft for a moment, and then started to put it aside.

There was a ghastly shriek, and a gray streak hurtled through the air, flying at the porcelain cat. The gray streak hit the porcelain cat squarely; it fell from the startled hands of the auctioneer's assistant and smashed to pieces on the floor. James fell sobbing onto the remains of his beloved. Pandemonium broke out. Lawrence ran to rescue what was left of the porcelain, and a guard came running to collar the cat.

13

However, it appeared that something was happening that was more significant than confusion over a rather unimportant piece of broken china. In fact, diamonds and rubies were strewn about the floor amid the shards of porcelain.

The auction was suspended for half an hour, and Lawrence Dobbs and I were asked to step into the director's office to wait for the police and the insurance executives to solve the reappearance of the jewels.

It was late in the afternoon when I returned to Baron's Chambers. James was lying in front of my door.

"Come in," I said. "You're a hero."

James heaved a deep sigh and dragged himself into the room.

I asked him if he wanted a drink, and he shook his head. He had destroyed the very thing he loved. There was no point in living.

I dropped the catalog for the second of the Haverstock sales on the floor, open to a page on which Lord Henry's fine Staffordshire cat was illustrated in full color.

"To bring you up to date," I said, "Lawrence Dobbs had had enough of being Lord Henry's secretary, and faked the robbery after putting the diamonds and rubies in cotton wool inside the hollow junk cat. Lawrence planned to buy it for next to nothing at the auction and then scarper to Brazil with the loot. If you had not broken the cat, no one would have been the wiser."

James turned to look at me, the look of a cat in agony, and then his eyes fell on the open pages on the floor. He jumped down and examined the color photograph that filled the page.

14

"Thwaite's thinks you're wonderful—though violent—and wants to give you something," I went on.

James was absorbed in the photograph of the Staffordshire cat. This cat was white with one black paw, and had gray eyes. James was alert again, and was patting the photograph softly.

"Lord Henry is so pleased with you that he wants to give you a home for life," I said. "But I told him you already had a home."

James flicked his tail. He was a changed cat. A keen intelligence gleamed in his eyes. He shook his head.

"Is there something you want?" I asked, even though I was beginning to guess.

James patted the picture.

"Your taste is improving," I said. "*That* is a classy cat."

James gave me an I-have-the-best-taste-in-the-world look.

"I'll see what I can do," I said.

Now, when I offered James a small drink, he accepted, and sat all evening looking at this new love. He occasionally licked the page.

At 10:00 P.M., Mrs. March came knocking.

"I've come for poor James," she said.

I looked over her shoulder to see James, alert and vigorous, sitting on the step.

"He looks fine," I commented.

"Oh, James, you are a one!" said Mrs. March as she scurried after him.

Lord Henry was delighted to give me the Staffordshire cat.

"Thanks to your cat, I have my gems back," he said warmly.

I didn't think it wise to tell him James was not my cat. Instead I thanked him effusively for the Staffordshire charmer, and carefully carried it back to Baron's Chambers.

James met me at the door.

He was frantic. He leaped into the elevator, clawing at the carpet. He streaked into the living room and, tail twitching, golden eyes glowing, he sat on the coffee table while I unwrapped the parcel and placed the white cat with the black paw on the table in front of him.

He collapsed in ecstasy. He patted, pawed, licked, and stroked the china cat.

"Have a drink?" I asked.

James hopped on the bar. His coat was fluffed up, his eyes alert. He whirled around to look at the table. The cat was still there. James drank his drink. He went into the bedroom. He came back immediately. The cat was still there. James beamed.

There was a knock on the door.

I answered it to find Mrs. March.

"Is James there?" she asked.

James jumped on the table, patted the cat, and then streaked past me out the door and frolicked up the stairs as Mrs. March trotted along behind him.

CHAPTER 2

A routine was evolving at Baron's Chambers. During the day, James supervised the maids and sorted the acceptable prospective tenants from those who did not meet his standards, and I worked at research. At about five o'clock in the afternoon I came back to Baron's to find James sitting on the tiny message table.

"Stop in for a visit?" I would ask.

After briefly considering whether there were any better offers, he would leap into the elevator, and when I unlocked the door to the flat, he would sweep into the apartment, inspect the premises, salute the china cat Lord Henry had given him, and recline on the couch, waiting for an exchange of gossip and a comforting drink after a hard day's work.

Sometimes I went out for dinner. Just before I was ready to go, at the most inconvenient moment James would tap haughtily at the door to indicate that he had an evening crammed with activities and that he had already given me more than enough of his time. I would drop whatever I was doing and say good-bye to James, who would nod graciously and sweep out into the hall.

On rare occasions I would invite James for supper. For these occasions I kept a supply of canned cat food.

James, who loves Laphroaig single-malt whiskey and

17

would turn up his nose at any ordinary whiskey—let alone vodka or gin—had, so far as I could tell, no taste in food. He was perfectly content with a can of cat food.

One evening we were sitting together, comfortably watching the news on TV. That is, I was watching the news and James was absorbing vital information with closed eyes, because, as I've previously mentioned, James, ever alert to the finer nuances of world affairs, finds it easier to concentrate if he closes his eyes. If I turn off the TV he will open his eyes with a start, look irritably at me, and wave his tail imperiously at the tube. So we were both absorbing world events when the bell rang announcing a visitor. We headed to the hall, where I responded to the security phone.

"Haverstock here," said a cheerful voice.

I buzzed Lord Henry in while James stretched and prepared to be his most aristocratic self.

Lord Henry, Earl of Haverstock, had become one of James's greatest admirers, and came to see him from time to time. Lord Henry is a short, muscular man with a gray mustache, ruddy complexion, and twinkling eye. At fifty he is the master of a considerable fortune and an impressive estate; he has been a widower for almost five years. He is shy, diffident, and sure he is inept. He is also intelligent, generous, and incorruptible. So far he has never found a woman to replace the first Lady Haverstock. He arrived this evening with a Fortnum & Mason shopping bag.

"What a splendid surprise!" I cried as we let him in. "What brings you around this evening?"

"Here," he said, handing me the bag. "I brought you something new to taste."

18

We set the shopping bag on the floor and unpacked a bottle of a new single malt, and two cans and a package. The package was from Paxton's and contained a wedge of cheese and some crackers. One of the cans contained Strasbourg goose-liver paté. I opened it and arranged the paté on some of the crackers while Lord Henry poured whiskey into two glasses and one saucer. To the glasses he added a dollop of water.

The crackers and paté on a plate, and the cheese on a board with a knife, were all on the coffee table, and we were ready for a delightful visit.

I reached out to pick up a cracker, but a gray paw intervened and a gray whisker brushed my hand. The dollop of paté on the cracker had disappeared. I looked at the bare cracker; James licked his cheeks and grinned.

"You like this stuff, old man?" asked Lord Henry. He offered James a cracker spread with paté. James nodded, his golden eyes glowing.

For a moment Lord Henry and I concentrated on an auction catalog of material in an upcoming sale. We were startled by an unexpected rustle. James was shoving the last of the paté in his mouth. Lord Henry had eaten one cracker with paté on it. I had tried but failed. James had eaten the rest, and looked blissful.

"James thanks you for the marvelous paté," I said with some irony.

James wobbled over to Lord Henry and offered his head to be patted. Lord Henry understood that this was a rare gesture of appreciation and patted the gray head vigorously.

Since there was nothing more to eat (James does not

consider cheese food), he began to entertain himself by jumping in and out of the shopping bag. At first he played at pounce, but before long the game appeared to have a purpose.

As Lord Henry prepared to leave, James jumped into the bag. Lord Henry picked it up and, talking all the time, we walked to the door. I opened it and said good-bye. Lord Henry put down the bag to shake hands. Then I turned to return to the flat. Grinning from ear to ear, James leaped out of Lord Henry's bag and scooted in the door. I heard him rustling in the bedroom, and before long he came struggling into the sitting room, pulling a Harrod's bag I had discarded. He gave me a purposeful look, marched to the pantry, and knocked the cat food off the shelf. Then he jumped into the bag and peered at me over the edge. An idea began to dawn on me.

"You like paté?"

A vigorous nod.

"You want to go shopping?"

James beamed; the idiot adult had finally perceived the obvious.

"Get in," I invited him. He did so. I went into the bedroom and got a scarf, which I tucked over him. He was hidden nearly completely.

"First thing tomorrow, we'll go shopping," I promised.

James sprang out of the bag and did little pounces of pleasure, but reverted to aloof boredom as soon as I opened the door and let him out. He met Mrs. Marsh on the stairs and ignored her completely. As she followed him, I could hear her admonishing him not to bother the tenants.

Next morning I was a bit nervous when I entered Fortnum & Mason carrying a Harrods shopping bag that weighed about ten pounds and was covered by a plaid scarf. Occasionally the scarf moved and a pair of golden eyes appeared, but no one seemed to pay any attention.

I stopped to look at what was available at the tea counter. The bag began to swing, hitting me in the leg. Being hit in the leg by a ten-pound weight will get your attention, and I moved on to the prepared-food showcase, which was filled with all kinds of wonderful foods: fish, smoked or made into mousse; game and liver patés of all kinds; and sausages, hunter's pies, deviled eggs, gelatins, custards, and so on.

I reeled off the list of what was available in a soft voice, trying to look as if I were unable to decide among all the offerings. The bag swung back and forth enthusiastically; clearly, James wanted it all.

I settled on a tasty and very expensive selection, and now, carrying not one but two shopping bags, made my way to Baron's.

I put the selection away in the larder and refrigerator, escorted a reluctant James to the door, and sent him about his business of the day as I went about mine.

That evening James insisted we open everything. He tasted it all, ate till his eyes blurred, and at last fell on the floor exhausted.

There was a familiar knock on the door.

"Is James about?" asked Mrs. March, peering into the apartment.

"Do let him spend the night," I begged. "I'm feeling lonely, and he is such good company."

"All right," said Mrs. March reluctantly. "But shoo him out in the morning."

James was not such good company. He had passed out from a surfeit of food.

In the middle of the night I was awakened by a firm pat on the shoulder. I opened the door for James, and watched him stalk purposefully out onto the moonlit landing, his tail twitching behind him.

When I opened the door the next morning to get my newspaper, there was James, sitting on a shopping bag. He dragged it in and with some effort got it upright, climbed into it, and waited, golden eyes aglow, for my response.

At first it looked like any ordinary shopping bag, a little the worse for wear. But from one side near the bottom a paw suddenly protruded. In two ratty holes near the top, on the opposite side from the paw, appeared two golden, gleaming eyes.

James hopped out, then hopped in, hopped out, danced down to the door, danced back, and nodded in the direction of the door. He was ready to go shopping again.

I got my coat and started out, carrying the bag with James inside, covered by my scarf. The bag banged against my leg.

"Stop it!" I said irritably.

The bag banged harder.

Really out of sorts, I put the bag down and addressed it.

"If you don't stop banging at me, I'll take you home," I said to the bag.

A paw came through the hole in the side at the bottom and beckoned.

I began to laugh. I had picked James up with his eye holes against my coat and his paw hole facing the world. Now I picked him up so that the eye holes faced the world and the paw hole faced me. I felt a reassuring tap on my ankle, and the bag remained stable. We started off again, found ourselves at the delicatessen showcase in Fortnum's, and I began to recite the selection. From time to time I would feel a poke and make a purchase.

The clerk grew restless.

"Sorry I'm so slow," I said. "I'm planning a small party and trying to guess what the guests would like."

"Thank you very much!" said the clerk icily.

"I guess that will do," I said with a sigh.

There was sharp poke.

"Something else?" Poke again.

"We now have salmon, game pie, a squab in aspic. Do you want liver paté?" No response. "Plaice mousse?" No response. "Deviled eggs?" No response. "Custard?" A fierce poke.

"Oh, yes," I said weakly to the clerk. "I'll take one of those custards. Please see that the cap is tight on the paper container."

"Yes, indeed!" said the clerk through his teeth.

Again I had two shopping bags. Everything was safely tucked away except the custard in one bag. I nestled the custard next to James's gray haunch in his bag, readjusted the scarf, and we started off.

The doorman saw us out. We started down the street, but something was wrong. The bag with James in it did not feel right. There was a tearing sound, and James and a plastic cup of custard fell out of the bottom of the bag.

Coming up the street waving at us was Lord Henry.

James had been dumped on his tail, and the custard, whose lid had not been firmly put in place, had spilled all over his back and haunches.

One of England's most aristocratic cats meeting his treasured friend and peer on the streets of London was not pleased with his predicament. Attempting some semblance of dignity, he stretched his back and raised his head. The custard ran down his legs, a sticky, creamy mess.

"I say, what an accident!" cried Lord Henry, stooping to pick up the custard and salvage what was possible. He, too, is an aristocrat, and knows instinctively that one does not laugh at a peer in trouble, whatever the provocation.

James saluted his friend with a gesture that seemed to say, "Everyone is soaked with vanilla custard every day."

And so, with Lord Henry carrying a sticky, half-filled cup of custard, James stalking ahead with creamy custard running down his hind leg, and me bringing up the rear, carrying two bags, one full of food and the other with the bottom out of it, dragging a plaid scarf behind, we proceeded to Baron's.

Once safely in the apartment, Lord Henry stowed the provisions in the larder and refrigerator. James permitted himself to be wiped off and was forced to clean himself while trying to pretend the whole disgraceful episode had never happened.

While I was wiping the custard off James, Lord Henry was on the telephone.

"Got a tape measure?" he asked, holding his hand over the mouthpiece.

I had one, and produced it.

24

"James, old man, step over here for a moment," said Lord Henry.

James stepped.

Lord Henry began to measure him and report the measurements over the phone.

"Sit, James," said Lord Henry.

James sat. More measurements were made.

"Thank you, James," said Lord Henry. James acknowledged the thanks and went off to look at the larder.

"Now, when will it be ready?" a pause. "Within a week? Fine! I'll come in and get it." Lord Henry beamed. "I think they can fix you up splendidly."

I had no idea what he was talking about, but decided to wait and see.

It was time for all of us to go about our business, so James, now only slightly sticky, and Lord Henry and I left the flat. James returned to supervising, and Lord Henry and I left to inspect pictures.

That night we had smoked salmon with Laphroaig, and when Mrs. March came knocking, James was his usual self, so when she asked, "Is James here bothering you?" I could reply, "Why, no, he is right on the stair." And there he was, twitching his tail as if to say, "Come on, you foolish old woman."

Mrs. March scuttled away after him.

As the week wore on, a change came over James. He began to get fat. He had found that the world had not only special delicious drinks, but food as well. Great, wonderful varieties of food. He slowed down, purred more, viewed the news with his eyes closed, and did not demand that we go out as much.

One afternoon, Lord Henry arrived with a big box. Attached was a card saying, "For Sir James of Baron's."

James managed to open the box at last, and there inside was a wonderful contraption. It was a gorgeous carrying bag made of light, strong parachute nylon, bound in leather and cleverly constructed with holes big enough for paws all around the bottom, and holes big enough for eyes all around the top. A special flap could be draped over the top, and two long leather handles made carrying either by hand or from the shoulder easy. Emblazoned on the sides were the Gothic initials *JR*.

James stared; one might even say he gaped. He tried to jump in, but in the week he had been eating, he had changed shape.

He struggled, twisted, and turned, and at last got in the bag. With some effort, he then got out. He looked at us coldly. Neither Lord Henry nor I snickered. Lord Henry had to cough and brought out his handkerchief and covered his face for a moment.

James sat beside the beautiful carrying bag, his usual confidence deeply shaken.

He got up and looked at the larder. He came back and looked at the bag.

He stomped into the bedroom and jumped up on the dressing table, where he sat down and looked at himself in the mirror and patted his fat cheeks.

He stood up and looked at his side view. He made a visible effort to tighten his stomach muscles. The effort produced no visible change in his roly-poly shape. He sighed a deep, sad sigh, hopped down, and went into the bathroom. I followed. He stood on the scales, which read almost a stone.

"James," I said, "you can stay in Baron's Chambers and eat your head off, or you can slim down and be a traveling cat. Even if Lord Henry were to provide another bag, you are getting to be too heavy for me to carry."

He stepped off the scales, walked to the living room, looked at the bag, and went to stand in front of the larder full of cans of deviled crab, caviar, and patés of all sorts. Two great tears welled up in his golden eyes and rolled down his fat cheeks. With a sigh of resignation, he turned and, patting the bag in passing, headed for the door. I followed and let him out. He did not look back.

For four days I saw no sign of him.

Mrs. March seemed distracted when she came to collect the month's rent.

"James is not himself," she said. "He seems to be off his feed. He let that terrible Mr. Parsons stay. He eats scarcely anything, and refuses to use the elevator."

"I'm sure he'll be all right," I said, but I didn't believe it. I was really worried about him.

The next evening James was at the door. A new, slimmer James, more than back to his old fighting weight.

"Won't you come in for a little something?" I asked, delighted to see him.

James entered and went straight to the bathroom, where he hopped on the scales. Just over three quarters of a stone.

With a great smirk he trotted to the sitting room, jumped into the bag, jumped out, repeated the performance and then trotted over to the larder, which had been somewhat depleted, as Lord Henry and I had been nibbling at it.

With one swipe of his paw, he swept the cans on the floor.

Out, he indicated.

"Have a drink?" I asked.

A look of horror came over his not-at-all pudgy face.

"Well, orange juice, then?"

He nodded.

I settled with my drink, having given James a glass of orange juice, and was about to munch on some ripe Stilton cheese on a cracker. A gray paw intervened, patting the cracker and cheese out of my hand and onto the floor.

James shook his head and glared at me, then sat on my hands in my lap while we watched the news with our eyes open.

CHAPTER 3

Eventually James thinned down and lost his enthusiasm for running up and down the six flights of stairs that encircled the elevator shaft. Then one morning he greeted me at the door, and came in and patted the carrying bag to indicate that he was ready to try traveling in the great world.

His request coincided with my need to visit a friend, Helena Haakon, who lived in Brixton. She is a very talented artist who is struggling along doing occasional commissions and eking out her existence with casual jobs of any sort she can find, in between selling paintings or doing illustrations. I was researching a book for a client, and I knew the book would need some drawings, so I had called Helena—who could certainly use the job—and made an appointment for today. I decided to take James along to see her studio, and after making sure it was satisfactory with Mrs. March if I borrowed him for the day, we prepared to set out.

"We've a long way to go, James," I warned.

He only tossed his head, jumped in the carrying bag, and snuggled down while I put the covering flap in place. We entered the underground at Green Park station, and as we descended on the escalator I felt a sharp jab at my leg. I looked down to see that the eye holes of the bag were even with the sides of the escalator, and James was getting seasick watching them go by.

"Sorry," I said as I lifted the bag so that James could look down to the bottom of the escalator. I heard a deep groan. James had prepared himself for death.

The platform was crowded, and a group of young people were creating a disturbance to make sure we all knew they were alive. There was some jostling, and I was uneasy for James and tried to protect him from being bumped. Suddenly a girl with black lipstick and bright red eye makeup jumped away from me.

"That bag has eyes in it, and it hit me!" she cried.

People stopped and stared at the bag, which was perfectly still.

"Look," the girl said as she pointed from a distance. "There are real eyes in there, looking at me!"

"Come on, there's nothing there," said one of the boys, who had a safety pin through his ear.

"Well," said the girl, unconvinced, "I saw eyes in there, and they were fierce. Let's get out of here!"

The group moved to the end of the platform, as far away from me as possible.

A sign reading BEWARE OF PICKPOCKETS captured James's attention. He looked puzzled. I explained.

We got on the train, which was crowded, and to protect James from being squashed, I lifted the bag onto my shoulder.

Suddenly, next to me there was flurry of activity. The train lurched and a young man in jeans and a torn sweater began to swear. At the same time, something dropped on the floor of the car. There was more scuffling and bumping.

30

"Here, now!" cried a middle-aged man standing next to me.

The man stooped and retrieved what appeared to be his wallet from the floor while the young man in jeans waved his arms as though to fend off some stinging insects, and moved as fast as he could through the car to the other end. He got off at the next stop.

The passengers thinned out and there was room to breathe.

"I almost lost my wallet," said the middle-aged man. "That punk had lifted it, but then something seemed to bite him and he dropped it. I must be more careful in the future."

I heard James cough slightly.

"I'm sure you should," I rejoined. "We can't have guardian angels every day."

James purred.

In due time we reached our stop, after which we walked a short way through the busy streets and came at last to Helena's door.

She is a big, blond, handsome woman who loves animals, plants, good food, good drink, and all things beautiful—including people, whom she regards as, sometimes, the most beautiful animals she knows. Though she has almost no money, she never seems pinched or worried. She is full of love for adventure, and finds it in unlikely places.

Helena greeted me with pleasure and was delighted with James as he stepped out of the bag with great dignity.

"Oh, Sir James!" She welcomed him with a sweeping gesture. "The studio is yours."

For only a flash of a second he looked a bit bewildered, and then, rising to the occasion, he stalked around the studio, examining the easels and pictures stacked against the wall. Growing more interested, he burrowed into a pile of draperies in a corner, smelled jars of paint-brushes, and tapped the tubes of oil paint lying around. At last he jumped up on a big table where there were little dishes of colored inks, smelled them all, and leaped from there to a model stand, where he struck a pose.

Helena laughed delightedly.

"Before we do anything else, I'll sketch your portrait, you splendid creature," she decided.

The splendid creature swelled visibly and assumed his weary-of-it-all expression. Out of the corner of his golden eye he watched carefully.

Helena put a sheet of creamy paper on the table, and working fast and accurately, she inked in a powerful portrait of James. She used various brushes and colors from each of the dishes, washing one color out in a jar of water before using the next color. She concentrated entirely on what she was creating. No one spoke. James moved nothing but his eyes.

In what seemed to me no time at all, Helena stepped back from the table. "I think that will do it," she said.

It certainly would. A remarkable likeness of James, combined with an intense feeling for the catness of all cats, had emerged on the paper.

"James, you are a wonderful model," she said. "I wish all my drawings and paintings came that easily. We'll frame this for the exhibition."

With that, she took the portrait off the table and placed it on a drying shelf, then placed a fresh piece of paper on the table.

"What's this about an exhibition?" I asked.

"I have a chance at last to be seen with some classy company," said Helena. "Five artists are to have an exhibition at the Bosterson Gallery, on King Street, in about a week. I've been asked because Mrs. Bosterson hired me from time to time to serve at her parties, and got interested in me. When I run out of money, I work at cleaning or serving at parties or whatever turns up. In any case, five well-known artists had been asked for this particular event, and at the last minute one of them pulled out, so I got the chance to fill in. Of course, I was delighted. I will hang six pictures. I have four good recent ones. This portrait of James will be the fifth, and I'll do another in the next few days. It's a real break for me, because one of this bunch is very famous and runs with a crowd of theater and movie people. There will be reviews and all sorts of stuff. I might even sell one, who knows."

I told her how pleased I was as we moved into the kitchen, which also served as consulting room and library, to look at some examples of drawings that might do for my client.

"Good-bye, Sir James, we leave you now," said Helena, waving.

James nodded.

We sat at the kitchen table and concentrated on our business.

James jumped on the studio table and, twitching his tail in anticipation, dipped his paw into the red ink and then patted the paper. A red pawprint appeared. He fastidiously dipped the paw in the water, then shook it, and a shower of pink drops fell on the paper. He dipped his paw

33

in the yellow ink, patted again, and looked at the effect. He was delighted with himself. The more ink he got on the paper, the happier he was with the result and with himself. By the time Helena and I had finished our conference, he had created a collection of blobs, pats, sprays, drips, and scratches that covered the paper—and himself—with a riot of color. In the left-hand corner was scratched a shape that might be interpreted as a *J* if one were so inclined.

I looked in horror at the mess. Helena's fine paper destroyed. I was speechless.

Helena, too, was speechless, but for a different reason.

She spoke first. "James, that is just what I need for the exhibition." She laughed her wonderful laugh.

"Now, really!" I burbled. "This is carrying friendship too far. James has ruined your gorgeous paper, and I'll bet you don't have another sheet."

James looked at me with disgust.

"No, I'm not being nice," she said. "Mrs. Bosterson loves those paintings that are all splashes and splatters. I can't do them. They mean nothing to me, but she just might buy this one. I shall seriously exhibit it. Now all I have to do is frame these two, and I'm all ready."

Helena carefully took the spattered paper and put it in the dryer while James preened around the studio, totally unaware that his gray coat was spattered with multicolored inks. We three got ourselves together and headed for the nearest restaurant for lunch, where Helena and I ate curry and drank white wine, and James, who doesn't much care for curry, ate crackers and played games with his eye holes.

As James and I were about to leave for the station, Helena said, pressing into my hand two tickets to the opening, "If you come, we can sit in the corner and giggle at all the other people."

Of course, I agreed to go. James accepted with pleasure, licked Helena's nose, and we said good-bye.

James bounced all the way home. He played eye games with all the other passengers, and when we arrived at Baron's he did not wait for Mrs. March to pick him up, but bounded out of the bag and up the stairs, a great artist, fit and in full command of his talent, ready for anything.

Shortly after five in the afternoon on the day of the opening, James, no longer spotted but certainly ebullient, jumped into his bag, and he and I started off to the gallery, which was just around the corner. There we would meet Lord Henry, to whom I had given the other ticket.

Sure enough, there were lots of people and some reporters and photographers and a TV cameraman. We presented our tickets and, hoisting James up where he could see, I started around the first of two rooms. I thought Helena's pictures were far and away the best, but of course I was prejudiced. James permitted me to stop briefly at Helena's pictures, but he kept urging me on into the next room, and at last we got there through the crush to see Helena standing in front of the portrait of James, surrounded by a crowd of people and a cameraman or two. She waved and gave us her happiest smile. I was headed in her direction, but James scratched my neck, so I turned around, and there on the other wall was James's painting, matted and framed and looking like nothing so much as a colorful page of blobs.

Around me I heard, "Marvelous color." "Look at that subtle pattern." "A really profound statement." "How do

35

you suppose she did it?" "It's sumptuous." "It will knock the minimalists on their ear."

I began to chuckle when I heard someone say, "What a stupid picture! Pictures are supposed to be *about* something. I can't understand. How could a young lady like Helena Haakon let this get out?"

I quickly realized it was Lord Henry.

"Shh," I whispered. I put my mouth close to Lord Henry's ear, and in the confusion around us, I was able to say, "James did it."

"On the other hand," Lord Henry quickly recovered, "it has wonderful color and a profound message." Lord Henry could not bear to hurt his friend James.

James lifted his head out of the bag and acknowledged Lord Henry's compliment. At the same moment, Mr. Bosterson came pushing his way through the crowd and affixed a small red dot to the card on the wall that identified the picture. James's painting had been sold.

Helena came up with a reporter who asked, "What about this one? It's an entirely different style."

"I had a lot of help with this one from a friend," said Helena, laughing, and before I could stop her, she had lifted James out of the bag and draped him around her neck, where he sat looking regal. Flashguns popped, the TV cameraman took footage, and Helena and James posed. At last she returned him to me, and he rode on my shoulder while Lord Henry manned the carrying bag and we both drank champagne served by charming waitresses, and ate little sandwiches. James liked the ones with anchovies the best, and he adored the champagne. We all forgot about diets, and at last James, Lord Henry, and I reeled home, where James more or less tottered up to bed.

So the exhibition opened. There was a moment on the news that evening with James draped over Helena's shoulder, but this was far less important than the pictures of screen stars and the leading artist. The newspaper critics mentioned Helena in passing as a new talent, but that was all. One of her paintings sold—the painting James had contributed.

A week after the opening, a little group gathered in my sitting room for an afternoon something after a hard day's work. The group consisted of Lord Henry, Helena, James, and me.

Helena was not her usual bubbling self. "After one week, I've sold only one picture, and I had to cut the price in half on that for Mrs. B. There is no interest in me at all anymore. A one-day flash in the pan!"

I had never seen Helena so depressed.

James, who had been practicing painting gestures in front of the mirror over the bar, jumped down and came to sit on the sofa next to Helena. He gave her a rare affectionate lick on the cheek, and then, using a new strut he had recently adopted, he headed for the door as Mrs. March knocked.

The next afternoon, when Lord Henry came in, James came in with him, but paced back and forth irritably. Finally, by dragging both of us to the door, he indicated we were to go out right away. Out went, around the corner, and to the gallery on King Street. We omitted the carrying bag. James was a welcome visitor at the gallery. He nodded to the girl at the desk as we entered, and moved purposefully to his portrait. He leaped up on a chair placed against the wall near the picture, and, leaning over as far as he could, patted the identifying card. Then he got off the chair and patted Lord Henry meaningfully.

For a moment Lord Henry looked dazed, and then he began to smile.

"Of course," he said, and trotted off to the desk, where he and the young woman were in conference briefly, and she returned with him to affix a red dot to the card. Helena had now sold two paintings.

"The others seem to have sold almost everything? How come no one buys a Helena Haakon?" I asked the young woman.

"Well, you see, no one knows her yet, and everyone is afraid to make a mistake. Some people even ignore her work because they don't know her name. It's a shame. I'll bet if they took a little time with her things, she might sell a few."

James was listening.

The next afternoon there was no James in Baron's Chambers to greet me. There was, however, a small commotion up at the King Street Gallery. I went to investigate. Inside the gallery there were a number of people and some excitement.

A group was collected around one of Helena's canvases, and in front of them was a big silver cat, tottering on his hind legs, sweeping his front paws in a wide gesture that asked one and all to inspect the picture on the wall.

Of course, he lost his balance, but just as quickly regained his pose without any indication of confusion. After a few sweeping gestures, he leaped on a chair and patted the identifying card. Then he sat on the chair and glared at the crowd.

To my surprise, a fat man disengaged himself from the crowd and headed for the desk in the back, and the attractive young woman appeared shortly with a red dot and affixed it to the card.

James smiled a patronizing smile and left the gallery with great dignity.

I stopped to talk to the young woman.

"He sold them all!" she said in wonder. "He has worked that routine for the last three days. He did not always succeed, and it took him some time, but he insisted that people look at her paintings. His act amused them, and as a result the paintings sold."

"Does Helena know?" I asked.

"I'll call her this minute and tell her about the last one," said the young woman, and left me.

I walked home in a bit of a daze to find Lord Henry, Helena, and James at the front door waiting. We went into the building, rode up in the elevator, and entered my apartment.

I poured us all a little drink, and we sat sipping whiskey and eating some lobster paste I had laid in. I told them about the final sale and explained James's role in the event.

Helena picked James up and hugged him. James himself was torn between delight at being hugged by Helena, and distress that at that moment he had no dignity at all.

"Thank you. You are not only a great painter, but an even greater marketer," she said as she put him down.

James shook himself and tried to recover his world-weary expression, but failed utterly. Grinning, he turned somersaults on the floor and chased imaginary mice while we giggled and laughed until Mrs. March came to collect him. He was so ebullient he forgot his game and grinned at Mrs. March, rubbing himself against her legs.

"Aren't you the one, though," she said, blushing furiously, and they scurried away.

CHAPTER 4

As the days shortened toward winter, James settled comfortably into his wider life. He supervised the new arrivals at Baron's Chambers, checked out the Great Room at Thwaite's, and occasionally stopped by the gallery on King Street.

Sometimes, safely tucked in the carrying bag, he went with me to see Helena, who was working in her studio on an illustration commission that had come her way after the exhibition.

Often Lord Henry, Helena, and I would meet at Baron's for a drink and a chat before James went home to Mrs. March, and the rest of us went out to dinner.

One blustery afternoon, James sat on the bar, occasionally lapping whiskey from his saucer, his eyes barely open, and Lord Henry sat disconsolately on the sofa, his usual enthusiasm gone.

"I have to go to Haverstock Hall for the holidays, and I'm not looking forward to it," he said.

I waited. Lord Henry is a shy man who talks very infrequently about his own feelings, though he is unusually sensitive to, and considerate of, the feelings of others.

"Well, it's this damned tradition I must keep up," Lord Henry went on. "Have to have this holiday wassail reception for the village."

He stopped again, took a sip of his own whiskey, and stared out into the darkness.

James slipped off the bar and hopped onto the sofa next to him. Abstractedly, Lord Henry lifted his arm and James slipped onto his lap.

Pretty soon, Lord Henry began to talk to James.

"Every year, we—my wife and I—used to open Haverstock Hall at Christmastime, and everyone in the neighborhood came in for a drink of cheer, carolers sang, and later, on Christmas day, we went to services in our parish church and joined everyone else in a holiday party. I played Santa and distributed small presents to the children. We loved it, and it seemed that everyone else did too. Then my wife died and my sister came down from her home in Scotland to 'help me out.' Instead, she took over." He shook his head sadly. "Oh, James, she is such a cold fish, and such a snob. Now there is no food and punch and singing. She makes everyone file in, receive an apple, and go home. I could do the whole thing myself now. It is nearly five years since my wife died, but I cannot dislodge Etheria. We don't go to church because she says it is inappropriate for us, as aristocrats, to mingle with the common people. I don't want to do any of it, but I don't know how to get out of it. In fact, this year I thought of asking her not to come, but she beat me to it. She's there now. After all, it was her family home too, once."

He stroked James and sighed miserably. James's scheming expression appeared. He patted Lord Henry softly and moved restlessly off the sofa as a knock came at the door. It was Mrs. March, but she did not make her usual remark about James.

41

"I'm going on a holiday over Christmas and New Year's," she announced. "I'm leaving everything in the hands of Mr. Merriwell, so you'll have nothing to worry about. If you need anything, just call him. Is James here, by the way?"

James was in his usual spot on the stairs, but his expression had changed drastically with the mention of Mr. Merriwell. He was snarling fiercely. He stomped after Mrs. March in a rage.

For the next few days, James was distracted and Lord Henry was depressed. Then a distraught Helena came by. The heat had failed in her flat, and no one could tell when it would be fixed. She was trying to work in gloves, and not succeeding. We all sat in gloom. On the floor was a copy of *Stately English Country Houses,* open to a picture of Haverstock Hall.

James paced the floor; at last he stopped, looked long at the picture, then jumped on Lord Henry's lap and tapped him sharply on the cheek.

"What is it, old chap?" Lord Henry asked.

James waved a paw to include us all, and jumped onto the picture.

"I say!" said Lord Henry, beaming. "The very thing! You will all come to Haverstock Hall for the holidays. Helena can set up a studio in the west wing, and James can take on Etheria!" Lord Henry began to chuckle.

Helena and I had no problems. We accepted immediately. James presented a problem. We would love to take him, but would Mr. Merriwell let him go?

There was a timid knock at the door. Mr. Merriwell, a small, pale man, stood at the door.

"Is J-J-James here?" he stuttered.

James hissed and arched his back, and his ruff swelled.

"Please, G-G-God!" prayed Mr. Merriwell. He looked terrified. James hissed again and bared his teeth.

"Would you mind very much if I borrowed James for a couple of weeks?" I asked, now sure of the answer. "You see, Lord Henry has asked him to Haverstock Hall for the holidays."

"Yes, indeed," added Lord Henry, who had joined me. "We will take excellent care of him, and return him safe and sound after New Year's."

For a moment Mr. Merriwell seemed stunned. James lunged.

"Oh, y-y-yes, indeed. I think that would be wonderful," Mr. Merriwell said hurriedly. James subsided.

"Splendid," said Lord Henry. "We'll pick him up tomorrow morning." James gave us a conspiratorial look and stalked upstairs, Mr. Merriwell following him.

And so it was that we four friends packed ourselves into Lord Henry's sports car (while all our gear was stowed into a station wagon driven by Lord Henry's chauffeur) and headed for Haverstock Hall, in Devon, in the cold and the rain, to deal with Etheria and Christmas.

We drove through the farmland that had once belonged to the Haverstocks, past the parish church with its graveyard full of Haverstocks, past the pub, the butcher shop, the grocery, and on to a pair of stone pillars guarding a driveway. After a rainy drive through a park, we finally arrived at a large, impressive gray stone house, a tiny part of which dated from 1530. Various Haverstocks had added wings and ells and fronts and backs over the years,

43

so the whole building had a sort of jumbled, messy look. It had an imposing façade with pillars and a long sweep of stairs to the massive front door. Out of this door a footman came running with an open umbrella, and ushered us inside. We entered a huge, walnut-paneled hall, dark with the smoke of centuries, from which rose the massive staircase. Lord Henry led us to the left, into a very large drawing room where a fire blazed in a stone hearth and shadows raced around the walls. The firelight glinted off the gilding on the woodwork, and sparkled in the chandeliers. Uncomfortable gold-and-white furniture was arranged around the room.

Coming toward us was a stout woman in a tight corset and a gray silk dress. She wore pince-nez glasses through which she peered with large gray eyes. The corners of her small mouth were pulled down in distress, and her chin disappeared in her scarf. Lord Henry's sister, Etheria, was taller than Helena and towered over Lord Henry, who seemed to shrink in her presence.

"Henry," she trilled in a high voice. Then she looked at the rest of us. That is, all of us except James, who had entered the room as though he owned it, and was, at the moment, toasting himself in front of the fire.

"Who are these people?" she snapped.

Lord Henry made introductions in a sheepish way.

She turned away to look at the fire.

"*What* is *that*!" she cried in alarm.

"My friend James," said Lord Henry.

"Well, get rid of it," Etheria demanded. She stepped to the wall by the door and pulled the bell.

It was answered very shortly by a white-haired butler.

"Wilson, get rid of that," said Etheria, pointing at James.

"Wilson," said Lord Henry, very firmly, "that is James, my very good friend, and he is to be treated as one of the family. Do you understand?"

Wilson nodded. "Of course, Lord Henry, and permit me to say welcome home."

"Thank you, Wilson, and will you bring some whiskey and something to eat to the library? We have had a long trip."

"Certainly, sir." Wilson bowed. "Your bags have been put in your rooms, and Johnson is unpacking now, so everything should be ready for you after lunch."

Wilson turned to Etheria. "Will you be joining us for lunch, Madam?" he asked.

"Good heavens, no," said Etheria in a disgusted tone. "I am having lunch with the Marchioness of Wilter." She turned to Lord Henry. "If you must have that beast here, keep it out of my way." As she made this last remark, James, looking his sweetest, rubbed himself against her legs and twined himself about her, mewing piteously.

"Agh," screamed Etheria, and fled from the room.

The library, warmed by a fire, was filled with comfortable leather sofas and chairs and plenty of books. We all had a drink and a delicious lunch served by Wilson, and began to feel better. James ate a sampling of sausage and lentil soup and lay on the sofa next to Lord Henry and took a nap like the rest of us.

In the next few days, James fell in love with Haverstock Hall, exploring it from top to bottom. Helena set herself up in one of the larger rooms in what she called the west wing, though it faced north, and Lord Henry and I took to cataloging the china in one of the pantries. On Sunday, Helena suggested we attend services at the parish church and meet the rector and see about reestablishing the old tradition. Lord Henry was delighted, and off we went. Etheria did not accompany us, but James did.

In fact, Etheria spent very little time with us. She was never at home for lunch, as she seemed to have a large group of titled friends who gave lunch parties. She was often home for dinner, but as soon as she entered the drawing room, where before-dinner drinks were served at her request, James with a sickeningly sweet expression on his face, rubbed himself against her legs, jumped on her lap, and attempted to lick her face. He tried his best in every way he could to show her his undying affection.

Etheria hated him. "Go away!" she would shriek. James was deaf to her pleas. We ate dinner in the formal dining room, all dressed in formal clothes. That is, Etheria was dressed in a formal gown, Helena wore a long peasant skirt and a sweater, and Lord Henry wore a velvet smoking jacket. Immediately after dinner, which James preferred to eat in the kitchen, where he had made friends with the cook, we would adjourn to the library to watch television, read, or talk. Etheria did not join us.

On Sunday, as arranged, we went to eleven-o'clock services in the parish church, a simple, old-fashioned stone edifice with a particularly handsome altar screen and an old vicar who greeted Lord Henry warmly.

"It's been a long time. We've missed you," said the vicar.

"Yes," said Lord Henry soberly.

During the service, the congregation paid more attention to us than to the vicar, and afterward an old woman with a red wool cap and a sturdy cane came diffidently up to Helena and me.

"You're a friend of Lord Henry's," she said softly. "Do you suppose you could persuade him to give out the small gifts we have for the children at the Christmas party? It would make it a real event and would mean a lot to the members of the parish. Sort of the way it used to be."

Helena smiled her glowing smile. "I'm sure he would love to. Just a moment. I'll ask him right now." And she left to interrupt the vicar and Lord Henry. She returned almost immediately.

"I was right, he would be delighted!" she told the old woman. "And may we all come to the party?"

"Oh, how nice!" cried the old woman, beaming. "Of course, we'd love to have you all, even the honorable Miss Haverstock, if she wants to come." The last was added without enthusiasm.

"I don't think she will want to come," Helena said encouragingly. "So you needn't worry."

Time, place, and circumstances were settled on the spot.

Helena and the old woman shook hands and we made our way through a crowd of children who had assembled, picked up Lord Henry, and started out across the fields to Haverstock Hall. James was confused by stubble, shrubs, rabbits, squirrels, and birds, and sighed as though he had suffered a severe travail when we at last reached the safety of the hall. He saluted Wilson with a cheery wave of his tail, and raced up the grand staircase.

We were not so lucky. Wilson told us there were guests for lunch, who were already assembled in the drawing room. Old friends of Lady Etheria, he indicated. We peered in, and suddenly Helena looked apprehensive.

"Forgive me," she said. "I really have work to do. Will you make my excuses?"

Of course we would. No one had mentioned this gathering before we left, but there was nothing for it but to go in and face the assembly.

Etheria introduced me in a sort of cursory fashion to the Marquis and Marchioness of Wilter, the Honorable Lucy Poole, who was a middle-aged woman in a lavender dress with a lavender face and almost lavender hair, and a tall woman in tweed who had been in church with us, but did not remark on that event. Her name was Fumia Wettin, and Etheria indicated that she came from a very fine family but had no title.

Lord Henry knew them all. He called the Marquis, who was a big, athletic man, "Bunko." The Marquis called Lord Henry "Punky."

Conversation was restrained, and drinks served sluggishly. Lunch progressed and we were treated by Etheria to a dissertation on the decay of manners, which was interrupted by a veritable explosion at the moment she stopped to refresh her throat with a drink of wine. Red wine was sprayed all over the tablecloth as she choked and shrieked intermittently.

The Honorable Lucy Poole was so unmannerly as to give a giggle through a mouthful of food, and was immediately attacked by a fit of choking and shrieking at the same time, spraying little bits of green parsley over her end of the table.

I intentionally dropped my napkin on the floor, and in stooping to pick it up, I looked under the long table-cloth to discover a pair of glowing golden eyes winking at me.

"Go look after Helena," I hissed.

I heard a sharp gasp from Fumia Wettin, and then silence.

The rest of the lunch was subdued, once the mess created by the two women was repaired. At the end of lunch, Bunko and Punky went to the billiard room, and with the excuse of work to do, I was summarily excused. I raced to Helena's studio. She was not there, but from the room next door, which served as a sort of storage room, I heard exclamations of delight. There was Helena, holding in her hands a wonderful velvet robe of emerald green. On top of the open armoire from which it had come sat at a grinning James. His explorations had borne fruit.

"It is gorgeous, isn't it?" she exclaimed.

James nodded.

"I think I'll wear it sometime, if Lord Henry doesn't mind."

James grinned. He looked his most evil. I thought he had something planned.

We had started downstairs for the billiard room in the late afternoon when we heard an altercation going on. Etheria's high-pitched voice was clearly audible.

"Henry, your behavior is a disgrace," she was saying. "You have a position to uphold, and you are simply paying no attention to the loyalty you owe your class. Everyone will think you are allied with the riffraff you associate with. I won't have it!"

We started to hurry on so as not to eavesdrop on this embarrassing scene, but James forbade it. He put his ear to the door. We waited.

"Etheria, this is my house, even if you are my sister. You do not need to take care of me any longer. In any case, I understand from Bunko that you are to be married to the Duke of Inverness shortly, and you will have your own castle, not just a stately home, and all the trappings you wish for. Why do you want to ruin my life?" He sounded very unhappy.

"Ruin your life indeed! I am simply stiffening your spine to make sure you uphold the standards of our dear mother," Etheria stated firmly.

"I see you don't mention our father, the late Earl of Haverstock."

"He was weak, weak, weak!" cried Etheria. "But Mother put up with him because she had vowed to, and singlehandedly she kept up the standards of this house, and so shall you."

We heard Etheria stamp out of the room, and, filled with sorrow for our dear friend, we scurried to the billiard room.

Lord Henry mentioned that he had had words with his sister, and that as far as he could see, we could not have an old-fashioned wassail party as long as she was around, though we could indeed do the children's party on Christmas. Lord Henry was not weak; he simply felt he could not make Etheria miserable in what had once been her house.

"We will have everyone in for the ritual apple," said Lord Henry angrily.

"But if Etheria weren't here?" I asked tentatively.

"Then we could do as we wished. But there is no chance of that. I shall just have to wait till next year. But that's why I hate to come here. I love the old house, but the villagers look on me as a snob now, and it is uncomfortable."

James had been pacing the floor, and suddenly he now slipped out of the room.

We sat quietly watching the news on the box and listening to the sound of the car being brought around on the gravel to take Etheria to the fête at Bunky's place. Lord Henry did not like Bunky much, and had declined the invitation himself.

Suddenly there was a terrible noise—shrieks, bangings, and general turmoil. We heard Etheria yelling at the top of her voice. There was much running around. We were frozen for the moment.

James appeared at the door and blocked our exit. His expression was unfathomable.

There was the sound of a siren. James let us out of the room, and we all hurried to the great hall, where paramedics were loading the substantial shape of Etheria onto a stretcher. She was shouting instructions at the top of her voice.

"What happened?" cried Lord Henry.

"I fell down the stairs, you fool," cried Etheria. "I think I have broken both legs and a hip. Careful there, you idiot, you have a very important person here," she shouted at one of the paramedics.

I was about to ask how this had happened, when a gray paw patted me sharply. I looked down, and James shook his head.

We watched the procession move out the door, Etheria shouting instructions, which the paramedics ignored, until she was swallowed up in the cocoon of the ambulance.

We stood stunned.

James did a somersault or two, and then walked with great dignity up the stairs. We followed him to bed.

The next day, Lord Henry had a long talk with the doctor, who reported that Etheria had indeed broken a leg, torn a ligament or two, and cracked a rib. He recommended that she stay in the hospital until after Christmas, and then return home. We greeted this news with a certain joyfulness.

"I wonder how she fell?" Lord Henry mused. "Not that a fall wasn't what she had coming, and she'll be right as rain shortly."

I looked at James. He winked and put a paw to his mouth.

I said nothing.

Preparations began of a very different sort from those envisioned by Etheria, who telephoned instructions to us from the hospital.

Cook brought out old recipes for cakes and pastries. Wilson concocted, with some modifications, a wassail drink that had been used in the time of Queen Elizabeth I. We moved the furniture in the drawing room around to provide cozy groups and to allow for a big buffet table.

Helena made decorations for the table, and we all went out to the woodlot and cut branches and holly and came back singing, covered with snow, faces glowing, happy it would be a white Christmas. While we were outside, James spent the time supervising activities in the kitchen and tasting everything. I noted he was getting stout again.

In the evening we played old children's games and laughed a good deal. An invitation had been sent to everyone in the village by word of mouth and through the church bulletin. The whole village took on an air of expectancy.

Of course, Fumia reported everything that was going on to Etheria, who called frantically at every opportunity, but we ignored her.

The day of the reception dawned bright and cold. The snow was crisp and still white. The hall was busy. The table in the drawing room was laden with all sorts of good things. A great silver bowl, full of wassail, was set up in the great hall. A Christmas tree decorated with ornaments found by James in a storeroom, and obviously accumulated over many generations, filled the hall by the wassail bowl. The treetop reached to the second floor. James had been invaluable in placing ornaments on hard-to-reach spots.

At last we were all ready for the first guest. James sported a bright red bow around his neck. Lord Henry wore a bright red vest and a sprig of holly on the lapel of his tweed jacket, and Helena wore the emerald green velvet robe with a white scarf around her neck; a wreath of spruce twigs with red bows crowned her golden hair. She looked like a princess.

People arrived in droves, and Lord Henry found himself inexplicably shy. He stood to one side, beaming at all the guests as they entered, but it was James who was the heart and soul of the party. With a sweep of his paw, a

53

gesture developed long ago for the art exhibition, he welcomed guests at the door. He offered punch, checked the buffet table, and indicated to the footmen when things were wanted. And he rounded up children who strayed out of bounds.

For a brief time, while their parents had some food, he entertained a pair of eighteen-month-old twins by doing somersaults and chasing imaginary mice. In fact, he chased one or two real mice that had ventured in, attracted by all the crumbs that were slowly littering the floor of the drawing room.

He was everywhere at once. Helena at last extracted Lord Henry from his corner, and the two of them walked through the rooms, greeting and talking with everyone.

The carolers arrived and collected around the Christmas tree. James raced through the rooms, alerting everyone that songs were about to begin. Those who paid no attention were treated to mild scratches.

The carolers sang to great applause. Then the whole house rang with "God Rest Ye Merry Gentlemen."

Suddenly the big front door was flung open, and there on the steps appeared Etheria, with her leg in a cast, supported by the Marchioness and Fumia Wettin.

"My God!" she exclaimed. "What goes on here?"

"Just a Christmas party, sister dear," said Lord Henry, who was now feeling not at all shy.

James stood thunderstruck as Helena stepped forward.

The Marchioness also stood thunderstruck. Suddenly she curtseyed to Helena.

Etheria looked on in surprise. "My dear Marchioness, what are you doing?" She said. "She is nothing but a piece of my brother's riffraff."

The Marchioness blushed deeply.

"Oh, Princess, I beg your pardon!" said the Marchioness.

"Princess?" Etheria exclaimed.

"Come in, come in," said Helena. "Let me help you to the morning room, where you can rest your poor leg, and I will tell you all about it." She took one arm and the Marchioness took the other, and they headed to the morning room, to the right of the great hall.

As she left, Helena called out, "The party is not over. Please forgive me for just a minute." James dashed into action, and Lord Henry and I followed suit.

The party was pronounced a tremendous success by all and went on much later than anyone had calculated. Finally the last guest said good-bye, urged on by a tired and cross James, who was chivvying him on his way.

We went in search of Helena.

We found her in the library, curled up on the sofa, looking into the fire. There was no sign of Etheria, the Marchioness, or Miss Wettin.

James, almost totally exhausted, had collapsed on her lap.

"You were wonderful, darling Sir James," she said, stroking him affectionately. He purred.

"It was a wonderful party, wasn't it?" said a delighted Lord Henry. "It is without a doubt the best Christmas party we ever gave. The old hall has never been so merry. And what do we have to thank but that unlucky-for-her, lucky-for-us chance that sent Etheria down the stairs."

I looked hard at James, but he refused to meet my eyes.

"Now what's all this about a princess, and where is Etheria?"

"You see," said Helena, "my mother was the daughter of a German royal family, and she—my mother that is—married a Swedish nobleman named Haakon. My parents are both dead, and I have nothing to do with titles and such. I live in England and am a naturalized English citizen, but the Marchioness makes a hobby of all the royalty of Europe, dead and alive. We met many years ago in Sweden, and she remembered.

"Etheria was so humiliated at the thought that she had referred to a princess as riffraff that she insisted on being taken to the Marchioness's house for the night. She will be on her way to Scotland tomorrow, and I doubt she will be back.

"I'm sorry, Lord Henry, I did my best to assure her it meant nothing to me, but she could not be stopped. Her maid, Mary Jane, packed her bags, and your chauffeur took them over in the wagon."

Lord Henry looked at her in wonder. She smiled her golden smile and said, "The party was wonderful, and tomorrow you play Santa at church. Now let's go into the kitchen and forage before we go to bed. I took the liberty of telling Wilson we could fend for ourselves tomorrow. The staff deserve a free day after all the work of today."

Lord Henry laughed. "I beat you to it," he chuckled. "Wilson must think we are crazy."

He took Helena's hand, and the tall princess and the short earl trotted hand in hand off to the kitchen, followed by a very distinguished, nearly exhausted cat and me.

CHAPTER 5

The Christmas Eve party at Haverstock Hall was acknowledged a huge success by all, and the part James played added to his already well-established self-esteem. He was beginning to feel omnipotent. He could do no wrong. The Christmas Day service at the church was filled with warmth and fellowship. In the afternoon in the church parlor, Lord Henry made his appearance as Father Christmas with a great bag of small gifts for the children of the congregation.

Lord Henry handed the gifts one at a time to James, who made his way to the appropriate child and delivered the gift with a wave of his tail.

Some of the children, enchanted by the sight of a great gray cat with bright red bow tied around his neck, tried to entice James into playing. Each child was treated to a fierce golden glare.

Early in the distribution, a young boy hid his gift and pretended that he was next. James passed him up without a second look and, on the return trip, retrieved the original gift from under a chair and, with a sneer, deposited it at the feet of the young boy.

Once all the gifts had been distributed, Lord Henry hoisted James on his shoulder and walked about to the strains of "We Wish You a Merry Christmas" sung by children and adults and accompanied by Helena on the piano.

Lord Henry, without his beard, red coat, and bag, returned to join the members of the parish in drinking mulled wine and eating shortbread. James, lionized, in his red bow, enthusiastically lapped up the wine and sated himself on shortbread.

Finally, with the snow falling around us, Lord Henry, Helena, James, and I headed back across the fields to Haverstock Hall.

First we all had a nap, and then, refreshed, we sat down to a dinner, prepared by Helena, of roast goose, onions, currants, and apples with bread dressing, oranges from Israel, and finally a flaming plum pudding with hard sauce.

In the week between Christmas and New Year's, Helena settled into her studio and worked every day on a series of paintings she hoped to exhibit in early February.

Lord Henry had decided to catalog some sections of the library that had been untouched for a generation, and I helped him.

James spent two hours each morning inspiring Helena, then took a nap and sometimes joined us for lunch at the big mahogany dining table, where Lord Henry, Helena, and I sat around one end and James occupied the other, while a footman waited on us all.

On other occasions he ate in the kitchen, where Cook tried out new tidbits on him. After another short nap, for James and sometimes Lord Henry as well, we all wrapped in coats and mittens and went into the village to get provisions, to see and be seen.

James was particularly proficient at being seen. Everyone in the village now knew that it was James who was responsible for Etheria's having retired to Scotland, and he was regarded with affectionate awe.

At the butcher shop he jumped on the counter and occasionally added his paw to the scales as meat was being weighed, wearing a wide grin on his face, or hissed as Helena suggested a "nice mess of tripe" for dinner.

At the grocer's he played tag with tiny lapdogs, and rolled oranges on the floor.

At the pub where we stopped for refreshment, he stalked down the bar, sampling beers. No ordinary cat would have been allowed in any of these places, but James was a local hero, so he was indulged and admired, and he grew reckless. Each time we went to the village, he danced perilously on mounds of grapefruit at the grocer's. At the general store he would disappear, only to be found grinning behind a box of detergent, to the astonishment of some unsuspecting villager. Everyone laughed and applauded. James was ecstatic. Lord Henry, Helena, and I were uneasy. We knew James had no sense of proportion.

The last Sunday we all went to the eleven-o'clock service to say good-bye for now to the church.

"Behave yourself," I told James fiercely as we approached the door. James twitched his tail and disappeared.

Helena, Lord Henry, and I took our seats in the family pew and watched as the processional came down the aisle: the cross, acolytes, choir, minister, and last of all James, head erect, tail waving from side to side.

The acolytes took their places for the opening rituals, and James lay full-length on the altar rail, from which vantage point he watched the congregation. However, the ritual bored him, and when the vicar ascended the pulpit for the sermon, James grew restless.

First he performed acrobatics on the rail. Some people tittered. The vicar gave him a stern look, but nothing affected James. He saw the baptismal font and leaped onto the edge. Then, rising to his hind legs, he tried to perform his two-legged dance that had served him so well in the gallery. The congregation was mesmerized. James was carried away. Perched on the edge of the font, he flung his forepaws into the air in a gesture of expansive affection for all his dear friends sitting rapt in the pews in front of him, swayed back and forth, and fell into the font.

He let out a shriek and tried to scramble out, dripping with holy water.

The vicar, who had admitted defeat early on, stopped his sermon and smiled wryly.

Deeply embarrassed, I hurried to the font, grabbed James, and hustled us both back to the vicar's study as fast as possible. He shook himself and began a concentrated overhaul of his gray coat.

"James," I said angrily. He stopped licking himself and looked at me. "That was unforgivable!" I went on. "You were rude to the vicar, desecrated the altar, and treated the congregation to a cheap show of flash."

I was just getting warmed up and was about to remind James in detail of the excesses of his recent behavior, but he jumped on my lap and gently tapped my mouth. He looked so sad and humiliated I could not go on.

It was cold, so I wrapped him in one of the vicar's old sweaters and carried him home, where he curled up in a corner of the library with a paw over his eyes, and refused either tea or drinks. He picked at his supper at the end of the table, and did not look at us once.

Helena tried to hug him, but he shrugged her off. The footman tried to tempt him with flan served with brandy sauce. He only hung his head. He was not worthy.

After dinner he dragged himself to the windowsill in the library, removed the roll of padding that was used to block the draft, and laid himself down in the cold.

"Come, James," Lord Henry said firmly, picking up an unresponsive cat. "Punish yourself if you want, but not your friends."

James retreated to a corner under the drapes as Lord Henry replaced the padding roll. He put his paws over his head and retreated from the world. The rest of us watched the news uneasily. By the following morning he was more himself. He supervised Helena's work, took his nap, and ate quietly at the table, but chose not to go to town. He sat in the corner, refused tea or a drink, and lay on the library table in the evening—not even permitting himself the comfort of the fire or a friendly lap.

New Year's Eve was upon us. The village publican had asked us to join the New Year's festivities at the Rusty Crown. There would be noisemakers and games, and we thought it would be fun, so we accepted.

But what of James? In his present mood he hardly seemed ready for a party.

"Will you join us?" Lord Henry asked him at about nine o'clock as we were getting ready to go.

James shook his head, sighed deeply, and gave us his I'm-not-worthy look.

61

"Darling Sir James," Helena exclaimed, "it won't be the same without you!"

James sniffed and covered his head with his paws. As we waved good-bye he stood in the door, the picture of depression.

The pub was full. We were swept into the circle of new friends, and before long were playing "horserace" with dice and pop bottles on a course laid out on the bar. Dart games were also in progress, and some people sang around a piano played by the vicar.

The door opened to admit newcomers, and I felt a soft paw on my arm. There beside me was James.

"Hello, old dear," I cried.

James looked apprehensive and laid his paw against his mouth to shush me, but he had been spotted.

"Well, James, going swimming soon?"

"Quite a baptism!"

"It was a fine dance, too bad you couldn't finish it!"

"Hello, wet cat!"

The teasing was good-natured. Though James did not find it funny, instead of staring evilly at his tormentors, he retreated under my chair, genuinely abashed.

"He's lost his giddy hubris!" commented Lord Henry.

"Will wonders never cease?" commented the vicar, and started another song.

Once the teasing stopped, James sidled out from under the chair, tried a spell on my lap, and at last slipped atop the upright piano and lay still, occasionally keeping time to the music with his tail. He was actually trying to be inconspicuous.

Just before midnight, Helena put a paper hat on him

and he gave her a melting look, but his self-confidence was gone. He remained quietly on the piano, waving his tail and looking for all the world like any ordinary stray gray cat.

Soon after midnight we all walked home. James and I climbed the stairs to our room while Helena and Lord Henry lingered in the hall.

I looked out the bedroom window at the moonlight on the snow. James sat on the back of the adjacent chair and gazed out at the snow with me. I stroked his head and he began to purr tentatively as we wondered what the new year would bring.

CHAPTER 6

We said good-bye to Haverstock Hall, and returned to Baron's to find Mrs. March with a fading tan.

Lord Henry had brought a number of bulky packages with him, and was occupied with the contents.

Helena was now at work on a series of etchings full of dancing snowflakes and moonlight.

I was doing tedious things at the British Museum, and a subdued James resumed his routine at Baron's, but without his usual enthusiasm. Something was wrong. He still supervised the tenants as they first arrived, but those who hated cats—whom he used to attack with overwhelming love and attention—he now only glared at. And a cat-hater who is only glared at by a big cat is perfectly content. Some completely unsuitable tenants slipped through his screening and some utterly despicable luggage went totally unscratched.

In fact, all the enthusiasm had evaporated from his life.

One morning a bored James slouched into my room as I opened the door to get the paper. He flopped on the sofa.

"You're not yourself!" I commented.

I got a languid nod in return.

The phone rang.

"Meet me at Thwaite's, the stamp department," said a jubilant Lord Henry. "I've found this old album full of stamps, and I want Peter Hightower to look at them."

"Can I bring James?"

"Fine."

"Wake up, James," I said, patting him affectionately. "We're off to Thwaite's."

In the Thwaite's stamp department, old postage stamps, envelopes, and all sorts of objects related to the transmission of information through the postal system are assembled for private sale or public auction.

We met Lord Henry, who was struggling with a large, old, tatty leather album, and we were ushered into a small office completely lined with books. A broad desk, exceptionally well lighted, was against one wall, and ensconced in a big leather chair, which not only swiveled but also rose and fell at the desire of whoever was in it, was Peter Hightower. He was a round, blue-eyed, nearly bald man of about seventy-five, with a mobile face that constantly twinkled and smiled. He probably knew more about the postal history of the world than anyone else, and what he didn't know he knew where to find out.

"Come in, come in!" he cried cheerfully.

Introductions were made; as Lord Henry recounted the affair of the stolen jewels, James nodded politely and then lay down in the corner and yawned.

Peter Hightower opened the album to disclose on the first page a lot of old red stamps attached to the page with adhesive wafers.

"At least they're hinged and not stuck down, that's a start," said Peter.

He took a magnifying glass and began to examine each stamp. His blue eyes began to gleam. Once in a while he would tenderly lift a stamp off the paper, separate it with a pair of large tweezers from the adhesive wafer that held it to the page, and put it to one side on the desk.

"These 'penny reds' were very early British stamps. They were printed from plates of two hundred forty stamps. As the plates were used, they wore down, and on occasion a new stamp impression was made in the plate on top of the metal where the old engraving had worn away. Traces of the old engraving still remained, however, and those stamps that bear both the new and the old marks are very scarce and very valuable to collectors. They are also very hard to see."

James stopped yawning. He slithered onto the desk and looked at the stamps himself. Peter Hightower took no notice of him, but, seeing that we were confused, he reached above the desk for a loose-leaf binder, which he opened to a greatly enlarged photograph of a penny red stamp.

"Here," he said circling the *o* in the word "Postage." "You can see that there are two black lines outlining the outside of the *o,* one fainter than the other. There should only be one. If you find two, you have a reentry."

"You have one here," he said, picking one of the stamps out of the special pile.

We tried to see the faint line, but without a strong magnifying glass we failed.

Peter Hightower returned the stamp to its pile, where James stared at it intently.

Peter turned to a new page and began to study it. So

did James. Suddenly a gray paw delicately tapped a stamp halfway down the page.

Peter turned sharply. James was sitting immobile. Peter picked up his lens and looked.

Then he lifted the stamp off the page, put it aside, leaned back in his chair, and gave James a long look.

James scanned the page. He delicately tapped a stamp close to the bottom. Peter examined it and put it with the small pile. He looked at James again.

"Any others?"

James shook his head.

"Hmm," said Peter. He examined the page himself. James had been correct.

He turned the page and leaned back in his chair, waving his hand to James.

"It's all yours," he said.

James studied the page and shook his head.

"Nothing?" said Peter.

Nothing, James indicated.

Peter gently closed the album and put it aside.

He opened a drawer and pulled out an envelope, from which he extracted two stamps that appeared to be identical. He laid them side by side.

"James," he said. "Are these the same?"

James shook his head immediately. The look on his face said, "Any fool could tell that!"

"Which one has two lines at the top of the number five in the right-hand corner?"

James casually gestured toward the stamp on his left.

Peter grinned. He tipped back in his chair and ruminated. Suddenly he sat up straight and looked hard at James.

"How would you like to work for me?" he asked.

James was momentarily taken aback, then he sighed and leaped into Peter's lap. The two of them grinned at each other.

"What are his favorite things?" Peter asked as James purred contentedly in his ample lap.

"Laphroaig whiskey, crab salad from Fortum & Mason—none other—and sometimes cream teas," I reported.

So, on Thursday and Friday afternoons, James left his post at Baron's and slipped through the delivery entrance, past furniture, pictures, and miscellaneous objects in the warehouse, and went to work for Peter Hightower in the big office, where together he and Marilyn looked at such arrivals as needed the eye of James the expert.

At six o'clock or a little before, James would scratch at the door of my apartment and enter, showing signs of exhaustion. If Lord Henry was there, James would give him a lofty pat and then collapse on the sofa, barely able to raise a paw to gesture imperiously for me to produce a whiskey. He would lap a little at intervals, and listen to our conversation with the slightly condescending affection of the great expert for the beginner. James was back in form.

Peter vastly enjoyed James. James regarded Peter with awe.

Sometimes James left Baron's early on a Thursday, and he and Peter had crab salad and champagne for lunch at Peter's desk. Then Peter closed the door and he and James made the chair go up and down and then had a nap before tackling the day's consignment.

On occasion there was time for conversation.

Peter would tell stories, and James would listen and purr.

James turned out to have an exceptionately discriminating eye, and there was no one better at detecting forgeries.

Meanwhile, Peter trained James. Lord Henry acquired an increasing enthusiasm for the stamps and envelopes lying around in old trunks in Haverstock Hall. In fact, he was becoming a collector.

He had acquired albums, sorted the material, and found he had a good start toward a collection of Turkish stamps, as an aunt had adventured into Turkey in late Victorian times and written everyone in her family all about it. However, the collection was far from complete, so Lord Henry began to haunt bourses and stamp dealers and go to auctions. He often took James with him, and on occasion James would tap him sharply on the arm as he was about to buy a stamp and shake his head firmly.

Then, mystified, Lord Henry would arrive to see Peter on Tuesday or Thursday afternoon and discuss the stamp he had wanted. Invariably it was one that had been forged, and James had detected the forgery.

Meanwhile, at the upper reaches of Thwaite's, directors were simmering and soon they would boil over.

"That damned cat was prowling around the great room again!" stormed one.

"Break anything?" needled another as they sat at Silks, a restaurant across the street, having lunch.

"This is ridiculous. Suppose someone finds out we have a cat working—actually *working*—in the stamp department?" Said the first.

69

"I agree. You tell Peter Hightower where to get off," said the second director. "I'll hold your coat."

They drank a bottle of claret apiece in anger, and decided not to go back to the office after lunch.

Meanwhile, James had discovered another talent. His magnifying eyes were as useful in distinguishing between types of brushwork on canvas as they were at seeing reentries on stamps.

From time to time he would peer around at the paintings on view before an auction, and one afternoon, when there was little for him to do in the stamp department, he examined a consignment of fine paintings by John Constable that had just been accepted for auction and put on view. The catalog was printed, and the art department was ready to publicize a major event.

James looked casually at the paintings lined up on the floor, waiting to be hung, while Peter, Lord Henry, and I chatted with a couple of men from the art department.

James paraded in front of the pictures, then stopped and looked seriously at each one. Finally he stopped before a gray-green landscape and looked hard. At last he stepped next to Peter and tapped him on the leg.

Peter looked down questioningly.

James stepped smartly up to the landscape, extended his paw, and shook his head.

Peter nodded imperceptibly.

"Thank you very much," he said softly, apparently to no one. After all, one does not talk to cats.

A senior director came through the big room.

"I see that damned cat is still here!" he exclaimed, taking a swipe at James, whose dignity remained intact as he avoided the extended leg.

"Yes, I'm happy to say he is," said Peter.

I felt a little thrill of excitement.

"By the way," Peter said, having developed a sudden interest in the Constables, "what can you tell me about these?"

"Great find!" said the director, stopping. "I sent young Kirby around to get them as soon as Miss de la Rue called. We have known they were there for years, of course, but she has always wanted to keep them. Then, about three weeks ago, she gave me a call herself and said she was ready to part with them."

"How did she get them in the first place?" I asked.

"It's very romantic," said the director. "John Constable gave them to her ancestor at some time before 1811, and they have been handed down in the family ever since. We'll be delighted to be able to sell them, inasmuch as Constables are hard to come by, and there is quite a revival of interest in them."

"I see," said Peter. "And who checked them out?"

"Oh, our nineteenth-century English painting man, Tom Burke. He was very enthusiastic. Unfortunately he was called away two and a half weeks ago to care for his mother in Cornwall. The old lady has had to be hospitalized. Tough for Burke."

He turned to greet some new visitors.

"See you at the sale," he said.

"Surely before," said Peter. "Let's assemble in my office in about ten minutes," he whispered to us as he walked off to talk to friends.

Once James, Lord Henry, Peter, and I had crowded into Peter's office, we settled into a council of war.

71

"James tells me one of the Constables is a fake!"

James nodded importantly.

"Which one?" I asked.

"The muddy green landscape in the middle of the five on the floor."

"They're *all* muddy," grumbled Lord Henry.

Peter nodded. "I agree," he said, "but we can't let Thwaite's make a terrible mistake."

"Four of these paintings were given to a Miss Ellsworth by John Constable sometime in 1810, before his marriage. She was a student of Benjamin West, and she and Constable were friends and painted together sometimes. The pictures have been in her family, and greedy collectors have tried several times to get them, but till now the family refused to sell. We need to find out where the other one comes from and how it was misidentified. Tom Burke, Thwaite's nineteenth-century man, is one of the best in the business. He would normally never have made such a mistake."

"Are you sure James is right?" said Lord Henry. "Sorry, old chap," he added.

"Oh, yes, I'll pin my reputation on James," Peter said firmly. James gave his best friend, Lord Henry, a haughty stare.

We all sat in deep thought for some time.

"Why don't Helena and I visit Miss de la Rue, and see what we can find out about the odd picture," Lord Henry offered. "It is possible no one asked her."

"Splendid!" said Peter.

James, after a moment's thought, jumped into Lord Henry's lap and rubbed his cheek against Lord Henry's tweed jacket.

72

"You can come too," Lord Henry said. "In fact, if the weather is good we'll take a picnic."

James beamed.

"I'll hang around the office and see if I can find out what happened here," said Peter.

Lord Henry arranged an appointment with Miss de la Rue for the next afternoon, and he and Helena and James departed in the big, chauffeur-driven car for Guilford. The weather was terrible, but they took a picnic anyway, and ate it in the car, because James is passionate about picnics.

Peter asked around the offices and got answers, and so, in due time, we all met again at Baron's Chambers to pool our resources.

I poured drinks, Helena passed paté and brown bread, and Peter sat back in the big chair and began the report.

"Pure fluke," he commented. "Remember that young Tom Burke had to go to take care of his mother. It was an emergency, and it occurred in the middle of his examination of the Constables. He had examined three and put them aside. Then he answered the phone and heard the news about his mother so he called Bill Watson and asked him to finish the job, and then left in a terrible rush. Watson, after finishing what he was doing, went to Burke's office, where he saw two paintings on one side and three paintings in a group, and went to work on them, assuming that the other two were the ones Burke had examined. He then turned all five over to Burke's secretary saying they were all okay. Burke isn't back, and Watson has gone off to Birmingham on another job."

"What did you find out, Lord Henry?" I asked after we had absorbed Peter's information.

"More chance," said Lord Henry. "Miss de la Rue is eighty-eight years old and lives with a housekeeper in a cottage in Guilford, where her family has lived for some six generations. She is a charming, intelligent woman with splendid taste, but she is slightly deaf, and so fragile she can hardly walk."

"She had indeed sent the Constables off for sale?" asked Peter.

"Oh, yes, but she had asked her housekeeper to make the call because she has difficulty with the phone. In addition, when Kirby came, she was still in bed, and so she asked the housekeeper to get the five pictures from the dining room and deliver them to Kirby. Then she signed a receipt, but didn't look past the notation 'five pictures from Miss de la Rue.' She and Kirby never saw each other, so he never had a chance to talk to her personally. She is delighted that the sale is going through."

"Poor dear," said Helena. "She is the last of her family, and she wants to stay in her cottage until she dies. The money from the pictures will let her live in peace and comfort with her devoted housekeeper, so she is willing to let them go."

James was sitting on Helena's lap, and she stroked him softly. "She is so alert and interested in everything. I fell in love with her. Didn't you, James?"

James nodded.

"Did you learn anything more about the fifth painting?" Peter asked. He didn't like the idea of having to go to the director and say that James had discovered a Constable that wasn't a Constable.

"Tell them," said Helena to Lord Henry as she tried

to adjust a pair of spectacle frames on James's nose.

She and James went over to the mirror and looked at each other. "Because you're an intellectual cat," she said softly to him.

"It seems," said Lord Henry, "that Linda Ellsworth and John Constable used to paint together on Hampstead Heath in 1810. They often tried to paint the same scene, and discussed the theory of painting together. She was studying with Benjamin West and was reputed to have some talent, and one day she received a package and a letter." Lord Henry put on his glasses and very carefully removed from his pocket a letter sheet protected by a glassine envelope. The folded sheet was addressed to "Miss Linda Ellsworth, Hampstead," and contained the following letter, dated October 10, 1810:

Dear Miss Ellsworth,

It is with a full heart that I send you this package of four pictures. The times we have spent painting on the heath have helped me see what I want to do with my art, and I am deeply grateful for your interest and example. I do think your own painting is far superior to these, but perhaps they may bring you some pleasure.

With warmest regards, I remain yours truly,

John Constable

"So there you are," Lord Henry said, "four paintings by John Constable and one by Linda Ellsworth. You will notice that the letter sheet has three holes in it. That is because the folded letter was tacked to the frame of Linda's painting, where it remained until just the day before all of

75

them were picked up. In a moment of sentiment, Miss de la Rue took it off and saved it."

"She is happy to include the letter," added Helena, "particularly when she heard it might be necessary to identify the picture. We did have a wonderful afternoon, and James and I are going to call again in a week if we can get away. I want to take her a pulling from the series of snowflake etchings I did over Christmas, to replace the Constables. The vacant spaces on the dining room wall are sad."

The spectacles fell off James's nose, and Helena replaced them. "I think James wants to go, because there is a doll's chest full of clothes he has not as yet explored."

Peter began to smile.

"I think I've found the way out," he said. "I shall approach the director and hand him the letter. We will then find a frame with three tack holes, and in the process get Burke or Wilson to check all the pictures and see where we go from there. James need never to come into it."

James glowered.

"Really, old dear, we cannot have the world think that Thwaite's depends on a cat for its art expertise."

James was affronted. He rose to his full height, and with his head in the air he stalked to the door just as there was a knock. There was Mrs. March. James stalked past her without a backward glance and took his damaged pride out the door.

"Well, what happened to him?" asked Mrs. March as she followed him upstairs.

The next day, however, James had recovered his good humor, and he arrived in the morning to see what was up for the day. Since it was not his day at Thwaite's, he rode the elevator and looked at tenants while Peter took William Young, the director, to lunch.

"I have something difficult to tell you," Peter began. "There may be a question about one of the Constables in your upcoming sale."

"What can be wrong?" Young asked, and took a swig of claret.

"One of them is not a Constable at all."

"Oh, come now, both Burke and Watson agreed they were Constables, and there are no better eyes in the business." He took another swig.

"Read this!" Peter handed him the letter.

Young read the letter and looked at the address on the back. He handed it carefully back to Peter.

"Delighted the stamp department has such a nice piece. Should fetch a good price, with the Constable name in the news."

"But, don't you see, it means there were only four in the set," said Peter, somewhat perturbed.

"Silly boy," Young laughed. "How do you know he didn't give this Miss Ellsworth another, either before or after?"

"Because the picture is not by Constable."

"I suppose that cat told you!"

"In fact, he did."

"Oh, Peter!" Young was laughing heartily. "Have another claret." He poured Peter a glass and ordered another bottle.

Two men came into the restaurant, saw William Young, and came to the table. Introductions were made and pleasantries exchanged. The men moved off to their table with warm expressions of affection.

77

"See you at the sale next week!" said Young. "I know you'll have to have at least one of the Constables."

"I will indeed," said one of the men.

"Now then, Peter," Young said, after the men had left, "I appreciate your concern, but I cannot get excited about it. Just because you are getting old and have fallen in love with a cat, you need not think I have lost my head."

From Peter's point of view, the luncheon was a total failure, and with great misgivings he went back to his office, while William Young stopped at various tables at Silks to talk to collectors. Disaster was looming just ahead, in fact tomorrow.

We assembled to hold a council of war that afternoon.

"William Young paid not the slightest attention," Peter reported sorrowfully. "Told me I was old and had fallen in love with a cat. Which is true." He nodded at James.

"Come on," I said, Pollyanna to the last. "Let's go to dinner and hope for the best."

We all left the apartment, rode down in the elevator, and opened the door to the street. The cold air of late February hit us and we concentrated our efforts on getting to Franks nearby as soon as possible. We go often to Franks because it is nearby, very good, and James is joyously welcomed.

"Hello, hello," called our favorite waitress. "Where's James?"

James was nowhere to be seen. He did not appear during dinner. He was not waiting for us outside.

I said good night to Peter, Lord Henry, and Helena, and returned to my flat. No sign of James.

At eleven-thirty, Mrs. March knocked on my door.

"James here?" she asked, expecting to see him stride out.

"No, isn't he with you?"

"No," said Mrs. March. She was clearly worried, and so was I, but there was nothing to be done for the moment.

Next morning there was no James at my door with the paper. I talked to Mrs. March, and we decided that if there was no sign of James by afternoon, we would alert the police.

After breakfast I headed for the sale room at Thwaite's, for the sale of the Constable lots would come up very early. As I entered the building, I was conscious of an unusual amount of hubbub. Not only were a great many people coming to the sale, but there was an unusual amount of activity in the back of the sale room and in the halls.

The time for the sale came and went.

Finally, at about twenty minutes after the scheduled time for the sale to start, William Young took the auctioneer's gavel and pounded for attention.

"Ladies and gentlemen," he said, "I have an announcement to make. There has been an accident that has not only delayed us but has made it necessary to withdraw lot number ten, one of the Constable paintings to be auctioned today. We are sure it will be presented at another sale. Meanwhile, we will now begin the auction. I apologize for the inconvenience, and beg your indulgence."

He turned the gavel over to the auctioneer and left the room.

I spotted Peter by the door, and hurried to join him.

"The spurious Constable has vanished!" said Peter.

"Vanished?"

"Yes, the four were where they had been stacked last night, a little askew but safe and sound, and the Ellsworth was gone."

"So is James," I said.

We were both silent for a moment.

"Was there a break-in?" I asked.

"No, security is absolutely sure there was no way anyone larger than a cat could have entered and the door was opened only once after six for Tom Burke, who is back from taking care of his mother. There is no sign whatever of any attempt at entrance, and the guards were particularly alert because the paintings were in the hall."

In the background the auction was proceeding. Constables were bringing a lot of money today.

"What's everyone doing?" I asked.

"We've searched the auction room and adjoining offices to no avail. The police and our people are now combing the building. They started at the top and are searching relentlessly on the assumption that some inside thief hid the painting before he left for the night. But why that one?"

"Have you been to the stamp department yet?" I asked, as a tiny ray of light began to penetrate.

"No," said Peter. "With all of this, I certainly have not!"

"Let's go," I said, and hurried down the hall, which, in February, is dark even in the daytime. We passed executive offices and turned a corner. Just before the entrance to the stamp department was a utility room where a small refrigerator was used to hold milk and juice, a small metal table offered a place to prepare trays, and an electric kettle provided hot water. In a far corner was a sink with running water. I pulled the chain that activated the light fixture in the ceiling. The utility room was never locked. At first I noticed nothing but a roll of paper towels on the floor, but a tiny sound attracted me, and I looked under the table. There, fur ruffled as far as possible, eyes glaring, and teeth bared, was a large gray cat, sitting on a messy mound of paper towels. The cat hissed at me and suddenly stopped.

I backed out and shut the door.

"James is in the utility room, sitting on the paintings on the floor under the table," I whispered to Peter. "What do we do now? The search party will be here soon, not to mention the employees of the stamp department."

"Give me a minute," said Peter, and left hurriedly.

I stood guard. Marilyn and Fred appeared, herded by security guards. "We all have to stay here till the police have searched," Marilyn announced. I stood with them in plain sight, and no one paid further attention to us.

William Young came down the hall, which was getting very crowded. "Try that door," he said, pointing to the utility room, and before I could stop him, he had opened the door and pulled the light chain, and was facing a furious cat sitting on the floor, teeth bared and claws at the ready. Young lunged at James. James struck back, and Young retreated.

"Here!" he ordered a guard. "Get that cat!"

The guard tried to intervene, but the space was small and James fierce. I tried to intervene unobtrusively as best I could.

At last, Peter and Tom Burke arrived at the back of the crowd and made their way to the door.

"Thank you, James, it's all right now," Peter said softly, and James jumped lightly into my arms. Peter picked up the painting from under its covering of towels, and gave it to Tom Burke.

Marilyn, who had been watching, let out a little shriek. "James has saved the painting from a thief, and he's guarding it!" she cried.

I looked sidelong at James. He was smirking.

We were ushered past the auction room to the office of William Young, where we all gathered around to look at Tom Burke, who was looking at the painting.

Marilyn stroked James. "My hero," she cooed. "Imagine, he must have chased the thief away, and then he sat on the picture till we came. What a brave cat!"

I looked at James. James winked and then looked heroic.

Meanwhile, Tom Burke was examining the painting carefully.

"Where's Bill Watson?" he asked. "I want him to see this."

Watson was next door and, being summoned, he now appeared.

"Have you ever seen this before?" Burke asked Watson.

Bill Watson looked at the picture.

"No," he said, "I never saw this."

A few well-directed questions by Peter elicited the truth. The two men looked at each other, aghast.

"This painting is not a Constable!" said Tom Burke, after examining the painting further.

Peter nodded.

William Young groaned.

James purred, his golden eyes slitted.

Peter handed Tom Burke the Ellsworth letter.

"Of course," said Tom. "Now I see a tiny 'L.E.' in the lower right corner, almost hidden by the frame."

"I've heard about this Ellsworth," added Watson. "I was wondering why there were five Constables."

"We must look at the other one we missed," said Tom.

"I'm sure you must," said Peter. "But James said it was a Constable, so I for one am sure it is."

Tom rushed out to the auction room and returned with all the Constables. Some fifteen minutes of careful examination by both Wilson and Burke followed.

"All Constables as described," said Burke.

"I agree," said Watson.

The paintings were returned to the auction room. They had brought record prices. The Ellsworth was withdrawn without explanation.

The possibility of a robbery had alerted the BBC and ITV, and cameramen and reporters now crowded around to take pictures of the valiant cat.

The police continued to look for evidence of a breakin, but with the only object that had been disturbed now safely returned to its rightful owners, there was little else to do. At last, about noon, things settled down. The auction was recessed, William Young went off for lunch at Silks, and James, shepherded by Marilyn, ended up in the stamp department, where he and Peter had champagne and crab salad and a long nap.

As soon as I could, I called Mrs. March to report that we had found James, and he was safe. At five-thirty I picked him up, and we went back to Baron's. I poured him a drink, and one for myself. "All right," I said, "how did you do it?" James shook his head as if to say, "You are stupid." Then he pantomimed a cat tugging at the frame of a picture until he had dislodged it from the stack. Then he pantomimed a cat pulling and pushing and resting and pulling and pushing the picture down the hall, and pushing the utility-room door open. Then James jumped on a shelf and showed me how he had knocked off the roll of paper towels and wadded up paper on top of the painting to protect it. Then he sat on the pantomimed painting and looked smug.

"You wonderful old rascal," I said as I picked him up and sat him on my lap. We watched his performance on the evening news with our eyes open, and the rest of the news with our eyes closed.

When Mrs. March came to get him, he offered no explanation and walked out as though nothing had happened.

CHAPTER 7

The end of February was gray and cold, and there were frequent slush storms, wet snow that turned to rain or melted shortly after it fell, leaving the streets full of water. From time to time the wind rose and blew bitterly around the corners of the buildings, catching the unwary pedestrian in the grip of a frigid blast.

Lord Henry took Helena off to Gibraltar for a glimpse of sun. He had a strange patriotic streak that would not permit him to leave his beloved England in the lurch in bad weather, but after all, Gibraltar was a piece of England, so off they went.

When asked whether she would accept Gibraltar instead of Malta or Cyprus or Costa Brava or even Madeira, Helena had laughed happily and said, "Where thou goest, I go."

"Why don't you marry me, then?" Lord Henry had asked, not for the first time.

"I love you, but I can't marry you yet," was all she would say, Lord Henry reported to me before they left.

Things had settled down at Thwaite's. The Constable sale was a hugh success. The story of the Ellsworth painting had been retold a number of times in the newspapers and on TV, with appropriate pictures of James, looking competent or fierce as required.

No one had tried to change the general perception that the cat had frightened off some unknown felon. No mention, of course, had been made of his special abilities, or of his work with the stamp department.

Peter flew off to South Africa to examine the stamps of a South African who wanted to convert his holdings into money at auction, and would be gone for some weeks, so there was no one for James to play with at Thwaite's.

He dropped in as usual twice a week to see if Marilyn had anything for him to look at, but the cozy lunches were in abeyance.

So in the afternoon, in the drizzle, James and I sat alone in my sitting room, where we drank modest amounts of good whiskey, ate occasional dollops of paté, and read stories of cats in the news—which were infrequent, and so I took to reading him stories such as "Dick Whittington's Cat" and "Puss in Boots."

During the day, James returned more and more to his original job of inspecting the new arrivals at Baron's Chambers, an activity he had temporarily suspended during the great painting controversy.

Baron's Chambers was an old building, young by the standards of British history, but oldish in that it was built around 1750 and had been remodeled any number of times since. The walls were thick enough that it was hard to hear what was going on in other flats; normal TV and radio noise did not penetrate from flat to flat. The tenants, by and large, nodded pleasantly if you met them in the halls, and spoke gently, if at all, in the elevator. In fact, all of us, being well bred, tried to obliterate ourselves in the public areas of the building, thus the atmosphere was as close to silent as a well-disciplined group could make it. Of course, what went on inside each flat was none of our common business, as long as it did not intrude.

James, the careful observer, had an uncanny feel for the tenant who would be unsuitable and he had a number of techniques for putting an undesirable tenant off. If it was apparent that a new tenant with a reservation was a cat-hater, James would overwhelm him with affection, curl himself around the legs of the aghast prospective tenant, mew piteously, and scratch his luggage. Not enough to cause damage, but enough to cause anxiety. Often this alone drove the prospect to say he had changed his mind, and did Mrs. March know of a residence that did not have a cat?

Mrs. March generally did, and a telephone call arranged an alternative flat.

For really offensively picky clients, he had a special treatment. For those who wished to see a flat, he would slink along with the maid, slither into the bathroom as the client was inspecting the sitting room, and drag the towels to the floor, splash water from the toilet all over the bathroom, and leave dirty footmarks from the windowsill outside into the bathtub.

Finicky wives generally hauled their husbands out of the flat and out of the building posthaste.

However, these efforts were seldom required. The reputation of Baron's Chambers as a well-run, well-bred home away from home was solidly established, and only on rare occasions was it necessary to deflect an unsuitable guest.

However, it took vigilance. Once in a flat, guests were

hard to dislodge before they had to leave, so James had been in the habit of screening all comers with some care, except, of course, for the time he was spending at Thwaite's, or off junketing with Lord Henry, Helena, and me. More and more, tenants were arriving without ever seeing the great gray feline.

One day he found a middle-aged man wearing a dripping raincoat entering the elevator with a big, multicolored vinyl suitcase. James jumped in with him.

"Nice kitty," said the man in a palliative manner.

James glowered.

When they reached the sixth floor, James followed the man into the office and sat on the desk, glaring.

"Good morning," said Mrs. March. "May I help you?"

"Yes, I'm Fred Wilberforce, and I've come to join Bill Bummell in flat two," the man said heartily. "I thought I had better check in and get a key."

James shook his head.

"Of course," said Mrs. March. "Mr. Bummell has been expecting you."

James hopped off the desk and began to examine the large suitcase in detail.

"Nice kitty," said Mr. Wilberforce, as he tried to brush James away. James hissed, and Wilberforce withdrew his hand. The small office had begun to smell of very flowery after-shave.

"Just sign this registration card, and here's your key," said Mrs. March.

"Thanks, love," said Mr. Wilberforce in his loud voice.

James paced around in distress.

At that moment, Mr. Bummell appeared from the

fourth floor. James looked at the newcomer with interest.

"Scat!" said Mr. Bummell. "Get that cat away!"

James retired behind the desk.

"Mr. Bummell!" said Mrs. March. "I guess you never met James."

"And I never want to see him again," said Bummell. "Hello, Wilberforce," he added, slapping Mr. Wilberforce on the back. "Let's go."

I had walked up to the sixth floor to get my laundry from one of the maids, and I'd stopped outside the office, interested because James so clearly despised these two men. They paid no attention to me, but got in the elevator and descended to the fourth floor to enter the flat adjoining mine. James did not accompany them in the elevator, but watched as the cage left our floor, and his expression was not pleasant.

"Nice kitty," I said, and jumped out of the way to avoid a fierce swipe of a big gray paw.

An angry James trotted downstairs to the ground floor, where he took up his position on the table.

"Who are those two?" I asked Mrs. March.

"Mr. Bummell came in about a week ago, when James was spending all that time at Thwaite's. He said Mr. Wilberforce would be coming," said Mrs. March. "He is out all day, and for all I know, all evening as well. We never hear from him." She paused. "He certainly hates cats. I hope James will not give him a hard time."

I had a feeling James was out to give him as hard a time as possible, but I didn't say so. No need to make Mrs. March unhappy.

The first thing we noticed was that Mr. Wilberforce

89

and Mr. Bummell had very loud voices. They liked to kid around, and when one came into the building of an evening, the other, if he was home, would call down the elevator shaft. All six floors of Baron's Chambers would know what kind of a day Mr. Bummell and Mr. Wilberforce had had. Mr. Bummell liked to sing, and he had a loud singing voice that was slightly off key. His favorite song was "Violate Me in the Violet Time," of which he knew two lines, and often sang them as he left in the morning.

During the day, Baron's Chambers was respectably quiet. The rest of the tenants spoke in lowered tones. In fact, most of us had begun to whisper.

In the evening, however, things were different. Often both men would spend the evening together at the local pub and come home arm in arm, singing. They would crash into the entrance, howl with laughter in the elevator, punch each other affectionately, fall over each other on the fourth floor, forget to close the elevator door—so that it was immobile till someone came along and closed the doors properly—and finally collapse into the flat, banging the door after them.

There were no fights, only noisy conviviality. It woke the building and left the tenants angry. James was beside himself.

One dripping afternoon we sat in the sitting room. Or rather, I sat and James paced the floor. Clearly he felt something needed to be done. He left right after the news without a backward glance. At about one in the morning I was startled awake by a crash, followed by extensive swearing in familiar loud voices. The elevator rose to the fourth floor. Sounds of stumbling could be heard outside my door. Someone fell against it. I did not open the door. Mr. Wilberforce was laughing hugely. Mr. Bummell was cursing frantically. At last they slammed their door.

The next morning early I heard the flat next door being opened. There was a yelp and a scuffle.

"Help! Help!" I heard Mr. Bummell cry.

I opened my door, and there was Mr. Bummell in a pair of bright green pajamas. His face was red with rage and—could I believe it?—fear.

"That damned cat is in my flat!" he yelled. "Get him out!"

Mr. Wilberforce was sitting at the table in the sitting room, dressed in a red and purple striped dressing gown. The apartment was strewn with clothing, newspapers, and dirty glasses. There was no sign of James. He had disappeared. I was not surprised.

"What cat?" I asked. "I don't see one."

"I saw him come in. I can't stand cats," cried Mr. Bummell.

"Come on," said Mr. Wilberforce, "he's gone, if he was ever here. Thanks for checking," he said, holding out his hand.

Mr. Bummell sat down and looked around apprehensively. He was indeed afraid of cats.

During the rest of the day, James sat in his usual place and supervised Baron's Chambers.

Late in the afternoon, when Mr. Bummell returned to this flat, I heard him stop off on six and shout at Mrs. March.

"Keep that cat away from me!" he roared. "A cat does not belong in a service apartment building at all, so keep

91

him up here!" He stomped down the stairs and slammed his door.

Some time later, James and I heard the two men leave their flat and stomp down the stairs together. Mr. Wilberforce was singing "Violate Me in the Violet Time" as they went. James sighed a deep sigh and curled up on the sofa for a nap. He wanted no reading, no whiskey, nothing. I patted him in an affectionate way, but he refused to purr.

His nap over, James asked to be let out long before Mrs. March came for him. He obviously had some plan in mind, but I had no idea what it was.

That night at about two-thirty, there was a terrible sound in the entrance. Part of the sound was in the form of a terrified roar from Mr. Bummell, part was a shriek from Mr. Wilberforce, and the rest consisted of howls and hisses—new to me and to all the rest of the tenants.

There was a lot of stumbling around and at last the two men reached their flat and slammed the door.

The next morning, as I left, I said good morning to a solemn James, who sat on the table, regarding his domain. On the table next to him was what appeared to be a white tablecloth in rather rumpled condition.

James was tired in the afternoon and took a nap. He left early.

That night, Mr. Bummell and Mr. Wilberforce stayed at home and played sentimental music on their record player. Thanks to Baron's Chambers' thick walls, we didn't hear too much.

The next morning I overheard the two men talking as they left the building.

"This place is haunted," said Bummell.

"Nonsense," said Wilberforce in his hearty voice. "You were just drunker than usual. It was only a curtain."

"A curtain that shrieks?"

"It was nothing, I tell you," said Wilberforce. "This is a good flat, the service is better than most, and I like the sitting room."

"It's haunted," Bummell muttered.

I did not see James at all in the afternoon. At about eleven that night, however, I heard the front door open as I stood at my own door. I was coming in after dinner. Wilberforce and Bummell were banging their way in as usual. An eerie howl rose from the hall, and the lights in the entrance were suddenly extinguished, except for the weak lamp on the table.

I heard the howl repeated. A heavy body hit the ground and Mr. Wilberforce said "Oh, Christ!" and ran upstairs.

The howl ceased. Wilberforce ran past me, fumbled for his key, flung open his door, and dove inside, slamming the door after him.

I walked downstairs to see Bummell slowly getting up off the floor, where he had apparently fainted. The light in the entrance was dim, and it was hard to see exactly what was going on, but it seemed to me that under a large lump of white tablecloth could be distinguished the shape of a large cat.

Together we rode to the fourth floor. I banged on his door, and Wilberforce opened it a crack.

"Here, take your boy," I said, and handed the tottering Bummell in.

All was quiet. I entered my bedroom and turned on the light. There, sitting on the bed, was James, grinning from ear to ear.

The next day, Mr. Bummell stormed up to the sixth floor and canceled the remainder of his stay. Since he had paid for a month in advance, he was demanding a refund. After checking the flat and assessing damages, Mrs. March happily handed his money back and wished him well in another apartment.

"I'll tell everyone I know that this place is haunted," cried Bummell in his low, rasping voice.

"Oh, shut up!" said Wilberforce. "Let's go up the street to the Cavendish."

They left with their big bags in the rain.

James moved purposefully to the entrance hall.

"I wonder what those two were afraid of," said Mrs. March. "There are no ghosts in Baron's Chambers." She was looking for something. "James," she said, "where's my white tea cloth?" Suddenly she turned to me blushing. "Imagine, talking like that to a cat. How could he know where my tea cloth is?"

"You never can tell," I said gaily, and went about my business.

CHAPTER 8

James was full of himself. He had developed a new posture. He lay on his table by the elevator at the entrance to Baron's Chambers, his tail fanned out against the wall to make him look as large and important as possible.

Mrs. March had installed a mirror across from the table in the only wall space available, so that the tenants could take a quick check of their appearance just before facing the world. It was contained in a gold baroque frame and so placed that if James stretched his neck slightly he could see himself. He did so frequently.

As the days lengthened and sunlight, when it appeared, grew stronger even though it never actually penetrated the window of Baron's, James fluffed his fur and turned his head this way and that, trying different effects of light and shadow.

Lord Henry and Helena returned from Gibraltar, she to her flat in Brixton, and he to his club. They both looked fit, but there was a sadness between them. They offered no explanations, however, and greeted us all with affection.

Peter returned from South Africa with a gleam in his eye and bulging cases of material to study, assign to lots, and auction off.

The far-flung friends gathered again in my flat, this time for tea, scones, Devonshire cream, and strawberry jam. It promised to be a memorable reunion, and in a way it was.

To begin with, James was impossible. Peter Hightower arrived first, and from the time he appeared, James paraded around the tea table. He bowed ceremoniously, a king deigning to greet his subjects. As each guest arrived, he indicated which chair belonged to whom, and at last he had us all arranged as he wanted, Peter and me on the sofa in the middle, and Helena and Lord Henry on either side, in the big chairs. After Helena had poured tea, he indicated by a sniff that it was not for him.

He knocked a tin of smoked salmon off the shelf, and slapped my leg until I got up and opened it. He gobbled up smoked salmon and Devonshire cream while we ate and chatted.

Once the tea was cleared away, he went around the circle, tapping each of us, and ended up on my lap. He pointed to himself, jabbed me in the chest, and settled down with a smirk on his face.

Peter began to tell us about what he had found in South Africa.

James jumped off my lap, assaulted Peter, and slammed a gray paw on his mouth. Then he returned to my lap.

Helena started to speak.

James glared.

"He wants me to tell you all how he saved Baron's Chambers," I said irritably.

James nodded, smiling.

I told the story.

When I was through, James lifted both forepaws to applaud himself, and fell off my lap.

The congratulations were warm and effusive, but they seemed not to be enough.

James walked around restlessly, posing before the mirror above the bar from time to time, interrupting whoever was speaking.

"You know, darling Sir James," said Helena at last, a little exasperation creeping into her voice, "if I didn't know you were the most wonderful cat in the universe, I'd say you were at the moment a nuisance."

James was stunned. And at that moment there was a knock at the door.

There was Mrs. March, with a tall, good-looking stranger.

"This is Mr. Wolf," said Mrs. March. "He says he has come to interview James, and since James spends all his time with you, I thought he might find him here."

James turned from the mirror over the bar and looked Mr. Wolf up and down. What he saw was a lean, tanned man of about thirty-five, dressed in a sheepskin jacket and well-worn blue jeans. He had curly black hair, gray eyes, and a clipped black beard.

"Come in, come in," I said. "We'd love to give you both tea or, if you prefer, whiskey. Perhaps Mr. Wolf could talk to James here."

Mr. Wolf walked in and smiled.

Mrs. March sidled in apologetically.

"I really don't want to intrude!" she said.

James gave her a severe look.

The rest of us were frankly curious, and since James would not let us talk about anything but James, we might as well see what was going to happen.

For a minute or so, James and Mr. Wolf eyed each other.

"Let me take your coat," I said. "Will you have some whiskey?"

"Tea, thank you," said Mr. Wolf in a firm baritone. "Whiskey spoils my creative perceptions."

James stopped posing and mulled over the phrase "creative perceptions."

Mr. Wolf and Mrs. March were provided with tea, and we all turned to Mr. Wolf. James draped himself over the coffee table and looked dignified.

"I'm a TV producer," Mr. Wolf began, "and I'm working on, among other things, a program for children based on the story of 'Puss in Boots.' We have the script and the cast, I am directing the production myself, and now all I need is the cat. I saw your cat when he appeared on TV recently in connection with the Constable matter at Thwaite's. He photographs well [James preened], seems intelligent [James nodded], and since the animal trainers I know have no appropriate cats at the moment, I thought I would look him over. If you are willing, of course," he added to Mrs. March.

James rolled over on his back, and waving his paws in the air, he grinned a silly, sappy grin at Mr. Wolf and then rolled off the table, jumped into Mr. Wolf's lap, curled up, and purred.

Mr. Wolf regarded him with pleasure.

"Is he trained in any way?" he asked Mrs. March.

"Good heavens! Not that I know of." Mrs. March gasped.

James leaped off Wolf's lap and on to the table, where he nodded vigorously.

98

"Roll over," I said.

James rolled over. Wolf watched.

"Sit on Helena's purse," I commanded.

With a flourish, James did as he was bid.

"Walk to the door," said Mr. Wolf.

James obeyed, looking over his shoulder with a smirk.

"Well," said Mr. Wolf. "He certainly does seem to take direction."

None of us said anything.

James returned to the coffee table, looked at Mr. Wolf, and proceeded to portray a range of emotions from fear through anger to ecstatic bliss.

Mr. Wolf let out a great booming laugh.

"You will certainly do!" he said, patting James affectionately but none too gently. "Now, Mrs. March, how much do you want for his services?"

Mrs. March, no longer apologetic, got up. "Mr. Wolf, let us go up to my office and discuss terms," she said. We all knew that Mrs. March would discuss terms very effectively.

"There is one problem, however," said Mr. Wolf. "Someone will have to come to the studio with James."

Mrs. March looked crestfallen. We all knew she couldn't leave Baron's very long.

"I'd be glad to go," I said. "I can fit my research around James's working hours, I'm sure."

"Good," said Mr. Wolf in his hearty way.

"If Mrs. March and I can come to terms, I'll see you and James at our studio." He gave me a card. "Day after tomorrow."

Mrs. March and Mr. Wolf left. Mr. Wolf, his jacket

over his arm, banged the door behind him. His powerful voice could be heard in the hall as he and Mrs. March headed for the sixth-floor office.

In the sitting room, James was beside himself. He rolled over, sat up, pretended to catch mice, walked on his hind legs on the back of the sofa, collapsed in Helena's lap, and purred like a giant vacuum cleaner.

Lord Henry brought glasses for us all, and a saucer for James, and we toasted the new TV star in Laphroaig and, it being that time, we all watched the news together with our eyes open.

Mrs. March and Mr. Wolf did come to terms, so next morning I bundled James into the carrying bag, got into a taxi, and at last arrived at the studios of Illusions Limited.

We were welcomed. The carrying bag was examined and commented on, and at last James and I were ushered into a darkened studio where we sat and watched the brightly lighted scene where half a cottage and part of a landscape were being photographed by two cameras.

A young woman came up to us and said brusquely, "I'll take the cat now."

She picked up James as though he were a lump of laundry.

James submitted, his eyes nearly closed, his expression grim.

"Animals again, ugh," said the assistant director, who was placing one of the cameras. In one corner of the studio the young woman was dressing James in a cape, a feathered hat with a wide brim, and a pair of boots with flared tops. Once she had him costumed, she returned him to me. James made no gesture, but hissed softly.

"Keep him under control," she said firmly. "We don't want him running around the studio. Perhaps you had better put him in that case thing you have."

I nodded and she left.

A young man with artificially yellow hair, dressed as a poor boy from sometime in the seventeenth century, appeared on the set, had his face powdered, and rehearsed, sitting disconsolately in the half-cottage.

"You are at your wits' end," said the assistant director. The young man sat on a stool, hung his arms between his legs, and looked depressed.

"Good," said the director. "Now we'll try to get the cat to run in and sit in front of you while we do the voice-over. Camera one will get a close up of the cat. Then you look a bit hopeful and we'll get the cat to run out."

The assistant director approached me.

"We want the cat to come into the cottage, look at Bret here, and then turn around and walk out. Can he do that?" he asked.

I looked at James. I had never given him a direction before, except for the afternoon two days ago.

James got off my lap and trotted clumsily onto the set in his costume. He sat down in the spotlight and shook his head.

"Come on, kitty," said the assistant director.

James glowered.

"Stupid cat," said the cameraman.

"Come on, what's-your-name," coaxed the assistant director.

James sat.

The yellow-haired boy came over and patted James.

James flared up and showed his teeth.

No one moved.

Mr. Wolf appeared out of the gloom.

"This cat is a total loss," said the assistant director. "He just sits there hissing, and his trainer is useless. I told you not to use animals. Animation is the way to go with this!"

"All right," said Mr. Wolf in his booming voice. "I'll take over."

"James," he said, "show us what you can do."

James looked around. Slowly he got up, then rose on his hind legs and walked across the set from one end to the other, holding his cape around him, his hat bobbling from side to side. Then he left the lighted set and found the actor who was reading the story while the actors pantomimed it. He patted the actor sharply on the leg.

"He wants you to read aloud," I interpreted. James nodded enthusiastically and his hat fell off.

The efficient costume girl rushed up and adjusted the hat.

"All right," boomed Mr. Wolf. "Bret, take your place, cameras in position, we'll run through it and see what happens."

Bret sat on his stool and put on his discouraged face.

A voice in the darkness read the narration, which said the poor boy had not eaten his cat, but let it go off into the world, where the cat had conned the local peasantry into thinking our hero was the son of a rich nobleman.

The scene opened. James, on his hind legs, his hat on one side, a grin of conspiracy on his face, strode into the cottage, where he patted the sad boy on the arm.

Bret lifted his head and, looking at the leering face of an energized cat, let out a gasp of horror.

"Cut!" cried Mr. Wolf.

James sat on his haunches in disgust.

"This cat is your salvation," said Mr. Wolf to Bret. "You love him. He is your last hope, not a snake."

"He scares me to death," Bret said sulkily. "Why do I have to be in this, anyway?"

"Money," said Mr. Wolf shortly. "Now act, if you can."

Mr. Wolf turned to the cameraman. "Take all the footage you can of the cat this time," he said. "I've no idea how often he'll do this fine act."

The reader read, James repeated his act with some additions, and Bret behaved adequately. Mr. Wolf beamed. The cameraman took pictures, saying nothing, and the assistant director sat in the corner and muttered "Animals!" to himself from time to time.

Thus began a profitable venture and a great friendship.

Certain revisions were made in the text, and each day the reader read, James acted, and when he was not on the set acting, he was sitting on a canvas chair provided for him with his name on the back, next to the one Mr. Wolf occasionally sat in.

James invented business for the cat, and when there was no place for the cat, James watched the pantomime of the rest of the story. When he felt it necessary, he tapped Mr. Wolf on the arm or ankle and shook his head.

Then Wolf would ask, "What should we do?" And James would demonstrate. Often his ideas were adopted, but not always. Sometimes James sat on Mr. Wolf's lap and purred. So did Mr. Wolf. A most unusual TV production was in the making.

When the shooting was over, James leaped into his bag, and he and I hurried back to Baron's Chambers. By the close of a working day, James was tired, and so he sat peacefully with us, drank tea or whiskey, and gave us all the benevolent smiles of one who lives in a rarefied world.

At last the day came when Mr. Wolf announced that the film was finished. James would be needed no more. There was some editing to do, music to be added where necessary, and general shaping up, but the filming was complete.

At the end of the last shoot, when Mr. Wolf cried, "Wrap it up!" Bret, who had never ceased to be afraid of James, hugged all the rest of the cast: the heroine, a yellow-haired girl with enormous blue eyes and a bony body that looked almost fat on film; the villain, an aging actor laced into a corset; and assorted townsfolk and farmers. The cameramen congratulated everyone, the assistant director said, "Thank God that's over," and Mr. Wolf invited everyone to a party at the Café Royal Grill Room that evening, where we would meet Mr. Totter, the financier who had helped raise the money to make the film.

"Could James come?" I asked.

Mr. Wolf laughed his great booming laugh, hoisted James to his shoulder, and marched around the set.

"Not only shall he come, but you and Mrs. March and Helena and Lord Henry and Peter Hightower must all come too! After all, James is our star."

I had hoped that James would smile modestly, but he

raised his paws over his head in a prize fighter's winning gesture and fell off Mr. Wolf's shoulder.

I got him into the carrying bag and both of us into a taxi, where James made so much racket in the bag that the driver accused me of being a Regent's Park Zoo employee, stealing a large ape.

Lord Henry and Helena were pleased to accept. Mrs. March had to decline, as she had three tenants arriving.

"Won't you need James?" I asked, remembering Mr. Bummell and Mr. Wilberforce.

"No indeed," said Mrs. March. "These people have stayed here for years because it's so quiet. Now go and have a good time." She patted James indulgently.

Peter Hightower had gone off to Plymouth to look at a collection, so at the appointed time, James, Lord Henry and Helena and I arrived at the Café Royal to find a party in full swing in the grill room.

The grill room of the Café Royal is a triumph of over-blown Victorian rococo. The walls are covered from floor to high ceiling in mirrors encased in frames encrusted with cupids, flowers, fruits, and perhaps even vegetables, all sculptured in high relief and painted in vivid colors that are reflected back and forth into infinity, together with the guests, waiters, and silver serving pieces.

For a moment James was bowled over, even intimidated, by the scene of all the joyful cast and crew sopping up champagne and chomping down the extensive buffet, but one ride around the room on my shoulder showed him the infinite possibilities for seeing himself repeated countless times in any number of poses, as many as he could invent. So he climbed the walls, waved from a cupid's fat behind, descended through grapes, roses, and wings to get a sip of champers, then up a swag of plaster ribbon to the top of the mirror, where he waved his front paws and beamed on us all. At last, growing slightly tipsy, he struggled down to the floor, climbed on the buffet, and went to sleep amid the little cheese pieces.

Mr. Wolf entertained Helena with funny stories about filmmaking, and Mr. Totter, a small, severe man with a monocle and gray spats, talked about money with Lord Henry, who drank quite a bit of champagne in self-defense.

At last, at about one in the morning, I put an inert James in his bag and said good-bye and thanks to the party, and invited Mr. Wolf to join us all for tea, drinks, or what you will. He agreed to come in a day or so with the news of the date when "Puss in Boots" would appear on TV. He also insisted on driving James and me to Baron's.

Instead of letting us out, Mr. Wolf came into the entrance himself, and James, now wide awake, jumped out of the bag and flung himself into the arms of Mr. Wolf with a penetrating yelp.

"Good old boy!" boomed Mr. Wolf, echoing through the six silent floors.

"Meow . . ." cried James.

"See you in a few days, you fine fellow!" said Mr. Wolf.

"Wonderful party," I whispered, hoping he would get the idea.

"Glorious actor," bellowed Mr. Wolf.

Doors began to open. I grabbed James under one arm and stuffed Mr. Wolf out the door.

Silence reigned.

James and I ascended in the elevator to six, where I surrendered him to a thoroughly awakened Mrs. March and descended to my own floor. Doors closed and peace returned.

The next morning found a phlegmatic James at his post, supervising arrivals with only half his usual concentration. In fact, most of the day he slept on the job.

Slowly things returned to normal, though I could see that James yearned for the excitement of filming.

Peter Hightower was still away, and Thwaite's did not need his expertise, so life was humdrum. Then, one afternoon, Mr. Wolf called to say he had news, and I corralled Lord Henry and Helena for cocktails that same day.

We were all assembled: Lord Henry, looking very fit in a new tweed jacket, and Helena, glowing with her golden hair in a fat braid down her back and wearing a simple dark blue dress that set off her golden skin. James ignored us and sat on the windowsill, watching the street for the arrival of his current hero, Mr. Wolf.

Suddenly he leaped off the sill and ran for the door of the flat. I followed and opened it in time to hear the front door of Baron's open as James streaked into the hall.

"James!" bellowed Mr. Wolf from the ground floor, his rich voice filling the elevator shaft and reverberating through the six floors.

"Meowww," cried James in response.

Mr. Wolf ignored the elevator and raced up the four flights, two steps at a time.

As he arrived at the door, James threw himself into Mr. Wolf's arms with delight. A flurry of excitement accompanied the entrance of man and cat.

107

That afternoon we all drank tea and ate scones and Devonshire cream and, for a change, gooseberry jam. I had opened a can of anchovies for James, but he wasn't interested.

He curled himself up on the arm of the chair in which Shep Wolf lounged. (His full name is Marion Shepard Wolf, but he prefers "Shep.")

"You see," he said once, "my mother's name was Ruth Shepherd. She was an heiress, and there were countless jokes about how the wolf courted the shepherd to get at the sheep, and I kind of fancy 'Shep' Wolf."

So there he lounged, grinning at us.

"The film is finished, and by a stroke of incredibly good luck, it is to appear next week."

He stroked James familiarly. James made his vacuum-cleaner noise. Helena beamed.

"Details," demanded Lord Henry. I detected a certain asperity in his voice. I suspected he was not all that pleased to see Helena beaming at this tall, handsome, ebullient man.

"It seems that BBC 2 had scheduled some show for seven P.M. on Thursday next—a week from today, to be exact—and two of the participants, an acrobat and an animal trainer, both coming from Turkey, have been held up somewhere, so a friend of mine put in the right word to the right man, and we were seen, approved, and scheduled just like that! There'll not be much chance for publicity, but the time is absolutely marvelous, of course."

"Let's all meet at Frank's for early dinner next Thursday, and come up here to watch," I suggested. Frank's is right around the corner, and James likes it.

"Wonderful idea," Shep cried, and rolled James over on his back and scratched his tummy. James snorted with pleasure.

Helena began to assemble her handbag, notebook, and drawing pen; she had been sketching Wolf as he sat, and she was now to leave. Lord Henry rose at the same time and moved to get her coat from the bedroom, but Shep leaped to his feet, dumping James on the floor, and got to the coat first.

"Can I take you home?" he boomed. "Or even better, take you to dinner and then home?"

"Thank you," Helena said, smiling. "I should like that very much."

Lord Henry looked taken aback and annoyed.

Shep flung open the door. "Bye-bye," he called, for all the building to hear.

The elevator doors crashed closed. On the ground floor, Shep called out "See you all Thursday!"

"Meowww," called James.

The front door banged. There was silence.

James and I returned to the living room. There sat a disconsolate Lord Henry.

James gave his old friend a shrewd look and climbed up on the sofa next to him, giving him a gentle pat.

"You see," said Lord Henry, almost to himself, as he began to stroke James gently, "Helena says she is very fond of me, and we do have a wonderful time together. She makes me laugh, and believe it or not, I entertain her. We both love the country and hate show, but she won't marry me because Etheria disapproves."

"I thought—" I began.

"I know all that stuff about Helena being a princess was a momentary shock to Etheria, but in the cold darkness of February, up in her castle in Scotland, she decided a Swedish princess living in Brixton and earning her own living as an artist would never do. In fact, Helena's successes have made it even worse. She's notorious because she's had some publicity. Well, I figured we'd wait it out, and now here comes Shep Wolf, who is everything I'm not—big and handsome and self-assured—and he sweeps her off her feet. I don't know what to do."

For Lord Henry this was a very long speech.

"I'm sure Helena isn't swept off her feet," I said. But Lord Henry did not look convinced in any way.

Shortly there was a knock at the door. It was Mrs. March, come for James, but she stopped for a moment.

"That Mr. Wolf!" she said. "He's a nice man and gave James a very good job for a while, but he's so noisy! Will he be coming around much? The tenants are all complaining of the banging around when he comes and goes."

She gave James a critical glance.

James got up and rubbed himself affectionately against his old friend Lord Henry's leg, and left in a dignified and self-contained manner. He had a lot to think about.

Mrs. March agreed that James could go to dinner, and was even willing to join us to watch the TV program. I agreed to try to quiet Mr. Wolf, and at last Lord Henry went off for a solitary supper.

The only event of any importance in the next week occurred when Helena took James to visit Miss de la Rue on a particularly brilliant day heralding spring.

Helena reported, when she stopped in after delivering

James to Mrs. March, that in response to her own re-counting of the behavior of Shep and James—accompanied by a vivid pantomime by an exuberant James—Miss de la Rue recounted in a more serious vein the austere, man-nered, and considerate behavior of the most famous prince she had ever known.

"James paid close attention, drank his tea silently, without a single slurp, and bowed good-bye with great re-straint," said Helena, laughing. "I'm sure Miss de la Rue was giving an object lesson, and I think we shall have Prince James for a while, till something else strikes him."

We laughed together at the thought of our dramatic companion.

"Now I must run," said Helena, getting her things together. "Shep is waiting. We'll see you tomorrow at Frank's at five-thirty."

Shep again, I said to myself. I was not pleased. I am devoted to Lord Henry.

On the dot of five-twenty-five, James and I left Baron's to go around the corner and up the street to Frank's. James was not cavorting; he was moving with great dignity. He bowed courteously to hurrying London-ers, who ignored him.

At Frank's he greeted Shep with reserve—not a single wild meow escaped him—and he ate his dish of spaghetti and meat sauce with great delicacy.

As Shep cuffed him affectionately, James raised his eyes and sighed a sigh that said, "Children will be rowdy."

Helena and I winked at each other and encouraged this new mannerliness in James.

Lord Henry, who is always courteous, considerate, and perfectly mannered, was his usual self.

I noted that James was watching him carefully.

A review of "Puss in Boots" had appeared in *The Times* that morning, and Shep had brought it along to read to us. The review was full of praise for the brilliant animal trainer who had managed to get such a rare and unusual performance from the handsome gray cat who was, without challenge, the star of the show.

James began to expand with pride, but remembered he was a well-mannered prince just in time.

In the next paragraph there was considerable praise for the director and his imaginative production, and Shep boomed his delight so that all the customers in Frank's gave us interested stares.

At seven we were all assembled, including Mrs. March and Peter Hightower. James was now adept at arranging the seating, and had made sure Lord Henry and Helena were next to each other on the big sofa. Shep had to be content with the biggest easy chair.

"Puss in Boots" read the title on the TV screen, and then appeared the grinning face of our James. The James on the screen slowly winked a conspiratorial eye, and James himself winked back.

Without doubt, James was in the same class as all the great hams of history. Though he had no voice, his pantomime was unique. The rest of the cast became a backdrop against which James played. When he was not on the screen the pace dropped, but Shep had wisely kept these moments to a minimum, and at the end of the half-hour performance, our group was weak with laughter. James had thrown manners away and was clawing Shep's denim shirt and howling.

As we watched, a star was born.

"James," Mrs. March said sternly, "you are cater-wauling!"

James stopped short, in mid-caterwaul.

"It is time for us to go," said Mrs. March.

James maneuvered himself off Shep's chest with considerable dignity, bowed to us all, and strode to the door.

"Cheerio, old star cat!" called Shep.

James inclined his head, lifted a paw and placed it before his mouth to indicate silence, then graciously saluted us all and strode off after Mrs. March.

CHAPTER 9

The excitement died down. Things went back to normal. Cat lovers wrote letters to James, which were read to him to his delight, but soon other personalities came along, and his star faded. Shep, who was planning any number of cat features, found funding hard to get, and negotiations took some time, so "Dick Whittington's Cat" was still in what he called "pre-production."

Among the letters James received was one from Miss de la Rue. She congratulated him for his performance in "Puss in Boots," but suggested:

"I hope, dear James, that while you are indeed a most successful performer under Shep's direction, you would one day consider playing a part worthy of your real talents. You ought to consider Bastet. It would be a great challenge."

We read this letter one evening when Lord Henry, Shep, Helena, and Peter Hightower were all assembled.

"Who is this Bastet?" asked Shep, scenting another possible show.

"Bastet was a cat god of the Egyptians," said Peter Hightower, who knows almost everything.

James plopped down on the coffee table, lapped a little Laphroaig, and looked off into the distance, his mind full of the possibilities of godhood.

Before long, Shep took Helena off for dinner. Lord Henry watched them go wistfully, and then he, Peter Hightower, James, and I all went to Frank's. All through dinner, James was abstracted, and as soon as we returned, he headed upstairs before Mrs. March came for him. In fact, he did not even announce his return to Mrs. March, so she came to my door looking for him, and she and I spend a futile half hour going from flat to flat. At last, completely mystified, we both returned to her office to find James curled up on the desk.

The next day he persuaded me to read Miss de la Rue's letter again. After I finished, he still looked somewhat puzzled.

"Do you know what a god is?" I asked. It was a stab in the dark, but I was getting pretty good at reading James's mind.

James shook his head uncertainly, as if to say, "Not really."

"Well, particularly with ancient people, gods were personifications of the forces that controlled the world. They had power and were regarded with awe and adoration," I said as a start.

James smiled a little.

"A god generally had a small or large temple and was treated with great honor. Gods were supposed to control the lives of people and be able to make things happen. People still believe in various gods throughout the world. None believe in a cat god at the moment, however, that I know of. The ancient Egyptians had lots and lots of gods, some with the heads of jackals, some with the heads of birds, and they did indeed regard cats as gods. They even mummified some cats."

James looked unhappy at the idea of being mummified.

"It's a fine old notion, but of course cats are not gods."

James gave me a very severe look, and I found myself saying, "At least I don't think so. What can I do for you, sir?" I added.

Suddenly I had an inspiration. "Do you want to see a cat god?"

James beamed.

The very next day we went to the Egyptian section of the British Museum. After doing a stint in the reading room, we went outside and sat on the steps and ate sandwiches, and then I stuffed James in the carrying bag and went up to the Egyptian section. I showed James some pages from the Book of the Dead that had small cats in them, and some sculptures of cats. At the end of the trip we stopped off in the museum store, where we found a reproduction of a black stone Egyptian cat with gold rings in its ears.

James banged my leg until I bought the little sculpture.

We took it home and put it on the shelf next to the Staffordshire cat Lord Henry had given us some time ago.

James was developing a new expression, one of meditation in which it appeared his mind was far, far away. He was not asleep, just concerned with cosmic problems.

After a while he began to pat the earring. Then he patted his own ear and gave me a sharp poke.

"James, I can't get you an earring. In the first place, you would have to have your ear pierced."

James's eyes grew big.

"Yes, a vet would have to poke a small hole in your ear to put the ring through."

James shook his head; that did not appeal to him. But two days later, when Helena came by wearing gold hoop earrings, James investigated, discovered these were held on by clips, and made Helena try one on him.

The effect was splendid. James did his "god" look. He sat like the Egyptian cat and twitched his head slightly and the ring swung back and forth.

He shook his head and the earring fell off.

He rubbed his ear. It hurt where the clip had pinched it. "I'm going to have my ears pierced next week," said Helena. "Want to come and have it done at the same time?"

James thought this over and finally nodded slowly.

"Good," said Helena. "I'll check it out with Mrs. March, but since I'll pay for it I'm sure she won't mind."

The following week, James, in his carrying bag, and Helena, in a new green suit, went to the doctor's and each had an ear-piercing job. James was not content with one, and had both done and came home with two studs, one in each ear. Helena said he was stoic and did not squeal once. I noticed he drank a little more than usual that evening, however.

That same evening, as Helena sat with James on her lap, she said "Shep is really a darling fellow, isn't he?" James nodded enthusiastically.

"He is very talented at what he does."

James agreed.

"He is full of fun and ideas, isn't he?"

We all agreed.

"Should I marry him? He's asked me."

James leaped off her lap as though she had pinched him, sat in his godlike pose on the coffee table, stared at her with a stern and glowering look, and slowly shook his head. Then, to be sure she understood, he returned to her lap, patted her sharply to gain her attention, and vigorously shook his head. Emphatically no!

"Right you are!" Helena laughed. And when Shep, bounding ahead, and Lord Henry, following diffidently, both appeared to take her to dinner, she turned them both down, saying only, "I thank you both for the invitations, but I shall spend tonight by myself." Then she went on her way alone.

Shep and Lord Henry looked at one another, a certain reserve between them.

Suddenly James turned playful. He pranced around, grinned at us all, cocked his head so we could all admire his ear studs, and at last, laughing together, we all decided to go to Frank's for dinner. It was a spirited evening. James teased the waitress, performed tricks for the other patrons, and generally extended himself to be amusing. At the end of the evening he attacked the bowl of chrysanthemums on our table. Taking a flower at a time in his mouth, he distributed one to each of the remaining customers. At last we trooped back to Baron's and went our separate ways.

James was now absolutely committed to godhood. First he must get some proper earrings. It was a weekend, and in the yard of St. James Church a market had been set up. I put James in the bag and off we went. However, once in the yard, where stalls were set up to sell all sorts of things—scarves, jewelry, clothing, watches, pottery—James could not stand being cooped up in the bag in the face of such an abundance of objects. He leaped out and began to roam around, but of course he was not tall enough to see the tables, and the owners were not happy to have a strange cat walking all over everything, so I ended up carrying him on my shoulders.

Finally we found a stall with earrings for pierced ears, and a suitable set of circular rings almost exactly like that single ring on the statue. I bought him a pair, and we returned to Baron's Chambers, where I removed the studs and inserted the earrings. They looked spectacular, and James paraded around the room, peered into mirrors, and generally preened. Finally, after looking at himself enough, he indicated that the time had come to go to Thwaite's and show off.

We trotted over to Peter Hightower's office, where he often worked on weekends. When Peter saw James he let out a great roar of laughter and said, "Come along. Our antiquities expert is here looking at a collection to be auctioned soon, and he must see this."

James, somewhat taken aback at being laughed at, nevertheless agreed, and off we went to the third floor, where, in one of the safe storage rooms, we found a number of men: Mr. Young, who greeted James with a smile but no warmth; a fat man with a pointed black beard who was examining some gold statues; and two or three other men who were watching him. Peter Hightower greeted the fat man and presented James with great dignity. "Ah, Bastet," said the fat man, also keeping a straight face.

"This is the cat that saved our Constables," said Mr. Young. "Peter Hightower says he's unusual, so we let him roam around. He has never done any damage and seems to have done some good."

"James has been studying Egypt," I said.

James had noticed that one of the tables in the room was lighted from behind, and he leaped on it and posed as an Egyptian cat. The light glinted off his earrings. He assumed his most imperious pose, and even the fat man was impressed.

"He certainly has the feeling of an Egyptian sculpture," he said. "Do you suppose James would consent to come and pose for a while at the showing of this material?"

He was asking me, of course, but James nodded vigorously.

Then he stalked the tables, looking at all the gold and alabaster objects lying there. He looked especially carefully at a pair of golden goddesses about a foot high. Finally he patted Peter on the arm and drew him to the two objects.

Peter called the fat man to look at the two goddesses. "Hmm," said the fat man, "these are really not a pair. I had better check them carefully. How did you know, Peter?"

Peter brushed this question aside. The conversation became general, and as I listened, I noticed one of the men who were also in the room looking at James with great concentration.

So James and Peter Hightower examined the objects laid out on the table. From time to time Peter would ask a question and James would nod "yes" or shake his head "no." Occasionally James pointed out something to Peter, who looked again at an object and then nodded his head.

There were a lot of people in the room and no one paid much attention to Peter and the cat except a tall, dark man who was dressed in an expensive suit that seemed to have been made for someone of a slightly different shape, and wore highly polished shoes and a bowler hat.

Mr. Young, who was surveying the room, noting possible big buyers, approached this man as he was watching James's every move.

"William Young is my name," said Young. "I don't believe we have met. I am the director of Thwaite's."

"Mahoud Poachway," said the dark man in a soft voice, never taking his eyes off James.

"Interested in Egyptian art, are you?" Young continued.

"Profoundly," Mr. Poachway answered with a sigh.

"Well, there is some very nice stuff here," said Young, looking around with a self-satisfied smile. An assistant approached and whispered in Mr. Young's ear. "Excuse me," said Young, and left hurriedly.

Mr. Poachway paid no attention, but approached the table.

"My Lord Bastet," Mr. Poachway breathed as he got close to James.

James turned sharply at the sound of his new name, which he had been trying out in his own mind at that very moment.

Mr. Poachway's already large brown eyes grew huge. He bowed his head.

"God of my city, accept my prayers," he said reverently.

James was intrigued. He nodded and smiled and patted Mr. Poachway on the arm. His earrings trembled.

"Dare I ask," hissed Mr. Poachway, "will you grace my shrine?"

James paused. He was not quite sure what gracing a shrine involved, but he was clearly in the presence of a man who idolized him on sight. This man must be very perceptive indeed. James, ever ready for adventure, nodded affirmatively without a further thought.

Mr. Poachway, stunned, stood helpless for a moment.

James jumped off the table, waved to Peter Hightower, and trotted purposefully for the door. No one in Thwaite's paid him the slightest heed. Mr. Poachway followed in a daze.

The two of them stood on King Street, Mr. Poachway in a trance and James eager for an adventure.

"How will I get my lord to my shrine?" Mr. Poachway asked the wind.

James tapped him on the ankle.

Mr. Poachway stooped down reverently. James jumped into his arms and then pointed imperiously at the taxis that filled King Street at that moment.

His eyes wide with wonder, Mr. Poachway flagged down a cab and gave an address on Effra Road in Brixton. The cabdriver looked surly but agreed. "Watch that cat," he said, and drove off.

In due time, the cab arrived in front of a seedy building on a rundown street.

Mr. Poachway, still reverently clutching James, paid off the driver and descended some stairs that led to a basement apartment. Over the door of the apartment was a sign reading THE TEMPLE OF BASTET. James noted that the small yard was full of weeds, the sidewalk cracked, and the dustbin overflowing. He began to have second thoughts.

Mr. Poachway unlocked the door of his basement flat and carried James into a hall that extended the length of the apartment. On the right was a single door; on the left were three. At the end was a window covered with bars, which admitted light.

Mr. Poachway opened the door on the right. "Welcome to your shrine, Lord Bastet," he said with awe, and carefully put James on the floor.

James found himself in a long, narrow room extending the length of the flat, and filled with folding chairs. At the far end, a long table was draped in some sort of shiny fabric. On it stood, in the middle, a pyramid with the top cut off to provide a sitting spot for a plaster replica of the cat with the earring. On either side of the pyramid were two tall tapers and a number of votive candles. A quantity of paper flowers—somewhat dusty—were distributed about, and an incense burner was at one end of the table. Directly in front of the pyramid was an empty brass bowl.

The whole room looked dingy in the light of the afternoon sun that shone in from the windows opposite the table.

James was not pleased. If this was a godly temple, it needed work. He marched the length of the room, leaped on the table, jumped to the top of the pyramid—knocking the plaster cat off in the process—and sat on top of the pyramid scowling.

Mr. Poachway, eyes wide with wonder, walked up the aisle between the chairs and prostrated himself before the altar, getting his suit dusty in the process. Then he got up and hurried out of the room. He returned a few minutes later, dressed in a long, flowing blue and white striped robe and a white turban.

He presented himself once more, touching his forehead to the threadbare carpet.

James, delighted with all this attention, gave him a haughty nod. Mr. Poachway backed down the aisle and left the room. James sat on the pyramid and smiled until Mr. Poachway was gone.

Once alone, James hopped off the pyramid and examined the room closely. There were a pair of windows at the opposite end, which were closed, barred, and looked out into a dingy airshaft, and all the chairs. Not a very prepossessing temple. James had had a much more exalted idea of the surroundings appropriate to a god. However, sounds outside sent him scurrying to his position on top of the pyramid.

The door opened and people began to file in. Mr. Poachway approached the altar, bowed to the ground, lit all the candles and the incense, and stood next to the altar, smiling and nodding to each of the members of the congregation. These members were young, middle-aged, and old, both men and women, but apparently all poor.

When the last person had entered, the room was almost full. Mr. Poachway motioned the last person to close the door.

The congregation bowed their heads and Mr. Poachway prostrated himself before James while the congregation chanted over and over, "Bring us your love, Great Bastet." Incense filled the air, and James felt exalted.

Then Mr. Poachway rose and, standing directly in front of James, faced the congregation. James hopped off the pyramid and tapped Mr. Poachway on the back. The congregation gasped. Mr. Poachway also gasped and turned around. James was back on the pyramid and pointing imperiously to a corner of the altar.

Mr. Poachway bowed and moved to the corner. From this new position he announced, "Bring your troubles to Bastet. She will advise."

It was James's turn to be surprised. "She?" Bastet was a goddess?

A young woman in the audience rose. "Great Bastet," she said in a troubled voice, "I do not know what do to. I want to marry Emil, but my family are opposed. What shall I do? Shall I marry him?"

Mr. Poachway looked at James and prepared in a dignified way to answer, but James, who approves of young love, nodded vigorously, opened his golden eyes wide, and grinned.

The mesmerized girl smiled and sat down.

"Thank you, Great Lord," she said.

Mr. Poachway was looking uneasy.

A man stood up and asked if he should invest in his brother-in-law's business. James scowled and shook his head. The man sat down. All manner of questions followed. James answered each as it occurred to him. Sometimes he nodded vigorously; sometimes he shook his head and occasionally waved a paw to indicate that he thought the question frivolous.

Mr. Poachway grew more and more restless. At last he stepped forward, bowed to James, and led the congregation in chanting, "Bring us your love, Great Lord Bastet, we prostrate ourselves before you." James loved the prostration part. Then the congregation filed past the altar, and the sound of metal could be heard dropping into the bowl.

Mr. Poachway stood at the front door of the flat and greeted each person, then he returned to the altar, bowed, took the offering out of the bowl, and headed for the door. James anticipated him and ran through the open door of the shrine.

Mr. Poachway was terribly nervous. Having a god running around one's apartment was very unsettling. James followed him to what turned out to be a kitchen, looked around, found it dirty, devoid of spirits of any kind and clearly without crab salad, anchovies, or even Meow Mix, so he tapped an empty dish and made a gesture of eating.

"My God," Mr. Poachway said reverently to himself, "needs an offering!"

He tried to prostrate himself in the kitchen, but the room was too small, so he simply stood and shook.

"My Lord," he said at last, "let me return to the shrine, and I will bring an offering."

James sighed. This idiot would clearly do nothing until he was left alone in the terrible kitchen, so he led the way back to the shrine and resumed his seat on top of the pyramid and then waved his paw to dismiss Mr. Poachway, who scuttled out as fast as possible, carefully closing the door behind him.

Soon he returned with a bowl filled with some sort of gray mush and a smaller bowl of milk.

"Delicious lentils, my Lord," said Mr. Poachway uneasily. He bowed again and backed out of the room.

Mr. Poachway did not return until late afternoon, when he removed the bowls—the milk was all gone and the lentils barely touched—returned the brass bowl to its place, lighted the candles and incense, and prepared for another service. He bowed constantly and looked in fear at James from time to time. James amused himself by glowering.

For this service the room was jammed with people. In the front of the room a young woman held an eight-month-old baby who was bored and crying.

James shook his head, making his earrings sparkle and attracting the baby's attention. It stopped crying. James waved a paw. The baby waved back. As the baby responded, the mother looked frightened.

Mr. Poachway came to the altar and made obeisance, and the chanting began.

The incense swirled around, the room grew warm. The congregation swayed in unison.

"Love us, O Great Mother Bastet!"

Mother! thought James in disgust as he watched the young mother struggling with her active baby.

"Help us, Great Mother," chanted the congregation.

This time Mr. Poachway did not attempt to stand in front of James, but now, when the supplicants rose to ask questions, he interpreted the answers, and his interpretations were quite different from James's indications.

A young man across the room asked, "O Bastet, shall I leave my home and mother and travel to another land?"

James, always in favor of adventure, nodded enthusiastically. The young man beamed.

Mr. Poachway interjected, "My Lord Bastet suggests

that a spirit of adventure is always welcome, but warns that leaving your mother could be very hurtful."

James had meant nothing of the kind. He began to resent Mr. Poachway, who seemed to be playing God himself.

Mr. Poachway grew more confident as the service progressed. James grew more irritated. Finally, when James had given clear assent to a request to divorce a nagging wife, and Mr. Poachway had interpreted this as a sign that James really meant that marriage was sacred, James stretched his neck and yowled as loud as he could.

The congregation was electrified, and Mr. Poachway, trembling, brought the service to a rapid close, chanting "Love us, Mother Bastet."

The congregation rose and started to file out past the altar and the offering bowl.

As the young woman with the baby approached, James leaned down and licked the baby's extended hand.

Mr. Poachway's eyes grew larger, if possible.

"You are especially blessed by Bastet herself," he said to the young woman. The baby giggled. The last communicant left. Mr. Poachway shut the door, came to the altar, counted the offering with a smile, bowed to James, and said, "I will present you with an offering almost immediately, my Lord!"

James decided to wait and see what came this time. He had no desire to go back to the kitchen.

Shortly, Mr. Poachway returned with a bowl with some yellow rice and a piece of something else in it, and a small bowl of what appeared to be Coca-Cola.

From his pedestal, James nodded curtly. Mr. Poachway left closing the door without a word.

It was now evening. James had been away from home for nearly the whole day, had performed as a god on two occasions, and had been bowed to by a large number of people. More adulation even James could really not accept. He was also very tired. He climbed off the pyramid, scrunched the shiny fabric covering the altar into a bed, and went to sleep.

The next morning he woke with the sun, paced around the room, and assessed the situation.

He was now truly a god. He had never been so revered or adored, and he was not likely to be ever again. When the chanting started and the candles flickered and the congregation bowed, he felt truly wonderful, but the rest of the time there was no one to talk to or play with, no place to explore, no good food, delicious whiskey, or champagne, no one to stroke or scratch—in fact, nothing to do but sit on an altar and give advice. Now no one even listened to his advice, but only to Mr. Poachway's. It was not an entirely wonderful life.

He heard Mr. Poachway coming, and leaped on the altar. Mr. Poachway bowed, produced more food, and commented to the air, "Two services today, one in the morning and one in the afternoon."

James grinned and began to plan how he would perform at these services. Two a day might fill his time very well.

At Baron's Court that morning there was great concern. James had been gone all night. After a thorough examination, William Young determined that nothing was missing at Thwaite's, nor was James hiding there.

By noon a conference was called in Peter Hightower's

129

office to review the previous afternoon. It consisted of Helena, Lord Henry, Peter himself, William Young with the Thwaite's security chief, and me.

"It seems to me," said Young, "that a Mr. Poachway and James disappeared about the same time."

"What does Mr. Poachway look like?" asked the security chief.

"He's tall, dark, and thin, as I remember," said Young.

"Oh, that one," said the chief. "I saw him leave in a taxi, with a big gray bundle under his arm."

"James has been kidnapped," we all said at once.

"Where does this Poachway live?" Young demanded.

None of us had any idea.

There was no Poachway in the telephone directory. There was no Poachway on Thwaite's lists.

Peter turned to William Young and said, "Call that inspector friend of yours at the Yard, perhaps he can find the cab that transported Poachway and his gray bundle."

William Young looked miserable. From his point of view, the longer James stayed away, the better. Besides, he did not relish being laughed at when he asked Scotland Yard to trace a cat, so he was resistant, but at last he agreed and went to his office to telephone. All we could do now was wait.

At Mr. Poachway's, James had been fed and the room arranged. The candles were lighted, and a full crowd of supplicants jammed every corner. There was the same chanting as before, and Mr. Poachway knelt and bowed to the floor while James made various noises.

Mr. Poachway called upon those members of the congregation who had problems to ask the Lord Bastet for help.

This time, Mr. Poachway stood to one side and not only gave his interpretation of James's responses to questions, but added occasionally a suggestion that he, Poachway, high priest of Bastet, was available for private consultation. In addition, when James, infuriated by a particular interpretation of his advice, yowled in distress, Mr. Poachway, bowing deeply, knocking his turban on the floor, would interpret the yowl as a reinforcement of his own statement.

This was no fun at all. Here he was, the god—or goddess—Bastet, mighty lord of the congregation, relegated to sitting on top of a cardboard pyramid in a dingy room, being taken over completely by his high priest. Changes would have to be made.

At last the congregation left. Mr. Poachway reentered, promising an offering and happily removing an overflowing bowl of coins and bills and closing the door carefully behind him.

"Another service this afternoon," he said as he returned with a bowl of tiny white grains in a brown sauce, with bits that appeared to be fish, and more Coca-Cola. James hates Coca-Cola.

James ate a little from the bowl, and paced the room in deep thought.

When the afternoon congregation arrived, he waved his paw like a cheerleader at the chanting, leaped off his perch, and performed all his old dances on the altar table.

The congregation was mesmerized, but Mr. Poachway seemed to have lost his terror, and to James's performance he kept up a running commentary leading the congregation where he wanted them to go. As the session grew longer, the room grew very stuffy with the odors of incense, sweat, fish, and cat offal. (Mr. Poachway had not realized a litter box was as necessary as an offering.)

Slowly James realized he had met his match. All this adulation was fine, but he was its prisoner. It was time to find another adventure. So he returned to his place on the pyramid and caterwauled.

Mr. Poachway rushed to the closing chant, crying, "Bless us, Lord Bastet," and the congregation began to file out, now dropping large notes in the brass bowl. It took some time, since there were twice as many people as had come to the first service the day before.

James waited till the last of the procession was passing by, then jumped off the altar, streaked for the open door, and—leaping between the legs of the final attendees—raced past the front door and across the lawn into the next dooryard, where he stopped to get his bearings. Then he headed for home, friends, and real food.

It was evening when a sad group—Peter, Helena, Lord Henry, and I—arrived at Baron's. I inserted my key in the door and opened it. As I did so, a scruffy gray cat came streaking up and slid in the door. James jumped on his table, and we all took turns hugging him, and then we all rode up in the elevator to the sixth floor to report to Mrs. March, and then down to four to assemble in my flat for celebrations.

Various reviving foods and drinks were passed around, and James gorged himself on anchovies and Devonshire cream while Peter Hightower reported on his afternoon.

"William Young finally got through to his friend the

Scotland Yard detective inspector, and after much joking about a lost cat, the Yard sent a circular to all the taxi companies asking for information about a man and a cat going anywhere about the time our guard saw Mr. Poachway leave," Peter began.

James stopped eating at the word "detective," and looked questioningly at Helena.

She reads his mind better than the rest of us, so she stopped Peter for a minute and explained. "A detective is a person who finds out things. Those who are criminals are targets of most detectives, but they find lost people or, like you, lost cats, or objects of value. They are usually very clever people."

James nodded and his eyes assumed their intelligent look, and he now casually lapped at his cream. All the anchovies were long since gone.

"In any case," Peter continued, after a nod from James, "no sooner had the request for information been circulated than a call came in from a cabdriver who had taken a man matching Mr. Poachway's description, carrying a big gray cat under his arm, to an address on Effra Road in Brixton. I asked him to come around to Thwaite's to see me. He did so immediately, and when he commented that the cat wore—or certainly appeared to wear—earrings, I knew we were on the right track. We drove out to the address, and there was, indeed, the Temple of Bastet and a frantic Mr. Poachway, searching for his god who had disappeared."

James looked a bit sheepish.

"Mr. Poachway and I talked a bit and I explained that James really was not Bastet, but a very intelligent and un-

133

usual cat." James nodded vigorously, and his earrings bobbled. That stopped him for a moment, and he hopped on Helena's lap and signaled her to remove the earrings. Godhood was being abandoned, for the moment anyway.

"However, I was no farther along, really," Peter continued. "I'd found where James had been, but not where he was now. I had the cabbie drive aimlessly around the neighborhood in case we might run across him, but of course we didn't, and at last I returned to Thwaite's, paid a huge cab fare, and found Helena and Lord Henry waiting for me. We sat around mournfully, wondering what on earth to do. The detective agreed to send out a general alarm for a gray cat wearing two gold earrings, but he didn't expect any results except a lot of calls from practical jokers. At last we came around here, and here you were! How did you manage?"

James only simpered.

Then, when Peter had telephoned the detective inspector to report the return of the cat, we all settled down to watch the late news.

When the news was over, everyone left, and soon thereafter Mrs. March's familiar knock sounded. When I opened the door, James, instead of playing games, saluted her warmly and trotted off happily.

CHAPTER 10

The following day, James was back on his table, or rather under it, observing unseen. He also seemed to be spending more than the usual amount of time checking out apartments, and in fact he found a pin one tenant had dropped off a nightstand, and returned it amid an orgy of thanks.

On one of his regular afternoons at Thwaite's, when James and Peter Hightower were busy sorting stamps, they were interrupted by a visitor.

Detective Inspector Home was announced. Peter welcomed him warmly and James examined him carefully.

"I see you found your cat safely," commented Inspector Home.

"Yes, he found his way home," said Peter.

"Well, my problem involves forgery. I'm told you people are unmatched at detecting stamp forgeries. I wonder how you can do on money?"

"Glad to try," said Peter, who suspected that Inspector Home was, in part, taking up his time as a reprisal for using the Yard's time for a cat. "Let's see what you have."

Home produced a five-pound note. Peter examined it, opened his wallet and took out a note of his own, laid them together on the desk, turned to James, and said, "Are these the same?"

James looked at the two notes briefly, and shook his head.

"Got another fiver?" asked Peter.

Home produced a note from his wallet and laid it next to the two.

"Which one is different?" Peter asked.

James patted the first note Home had produced.

"What part of the note is most distorted?" asked Peter.

James patted the upper left-hand corner of the bill.

Home whistled softly. He looked very thoughtful.

"I came here to scoff when you failed my test," he said ruefully. "Our experts, after a long session with a magnifier, came to the same conclusion this cat arrived at in a few seconds. I see why you wanted him back."

"We wanted him back because we love him!" Peter said indignantly.

"Well," said Home, "that may be. Now I have a real problem."

He pocketed his bogus five-pound note and his good one, Peter returned his note to his wallet, and the desk was cleared while Inspector Home produced a small stock book. On the outside it appeared to be a bound notebook, but it had, instead of the usual paper pages, cardboard pages fitted with four horizontal slots into which stamps could be inserted for safekeeping. The book had four pages, and these were, indeed, full of stamps.

"We found this on a man we strongly suspect of being a fence for stolen property. He was on his way out of the country when he got involved in a brawl. We have to turn him loose today if we can find nothing more than breach of the peace to hold him on. He claims these are mostly cheap stamps, part of his own collection."

Peter took the stamps out of the stock book, put the book to one side, and examined the stamps. James examined the book.

"Nothing out of the ordinary here," Peter commented at last. "All very ordinary stamps, most of them in ordinary condition. Value of the whole lot isn't over fifteen pounds, and that's being very generous. He picked up the book and started to replace the stamps.

James patted his hand.

"Something here?"

James nodded and laid a paw on the top of one of the cardboard pages.

Peter took out his magnifying glass and carefully examined the top of the page.

"Look here," he said excitedly. "This page has been very carefully slit and re-glued at the top."

Then, very delicately, Peter felt the page. "There's something inside," he exclaimed.

James nodded.

Peter produced a sharp knife and slit open the glued edges. He gently pinched the page and, using a pair of stamp tongs, drew two stamps out of the hollow space inside the cardboard.

"Well," he said, looking at them. "This is a different matter."

"What do you mean?" asked a very excited Home.

"These two are very valuable indeed," said Peter. "I think I know who they belong to. If I'm right, we'll have a real burglary on our hands."

"Marilyn," he called, "get Felix Benson on the phone, if you can." Turning to Home, he said, "These stamps, I'm sure, are part of a very fine collection belonging to Felix Benson. Felix has been traveling for the last two weeks, and was scheduled home late last night. I'll check with him to see if he has his copies."

"Mr. Benson on the phone," Marilyn announced. "And he's angry at being awakened."

"He'll be madder still, soon," said Peter, and turned to the phone. "Felix, Peter Hightower here. Did you have a good trip? . . . Fine . . . Not really up yet? . . . Would you check and see if your Mauritius collection is safe? Yes, I know it's silly, but please indulge me. I'll wait."

Peter did not have to wait long. A sputtering noise on the phone preceded an enraged yell from Felix Benson. "Four of my albums are gone! How did you know?"

"Never mind that now," Peter said. "Call your local police immediately, and be prepared to receive Detective Inspector Home from Scotland Yard as soon as he can get to you. You may be able to get it all back."

There was more sputtering. Mr. Benson was turned over to Inspector Home, and Peter gave James an admiring look.

Inspector Home gathered up the book and the stamps, all carefully placed in a protective plastic envelope, thanked Peter effusively, gave James a very puzzled look, and took himself off to solve a burglary he hadn't known had taken place.

"You'll never get the credit," said Peter to James, chuckling. "The Yard will never admit they owe this one to a cat, but we'll never have any more jokes from them, you may be sure."

James ruffled his fur and grinned. Being a detective was truly delightful.

That evening, James practiced slipping silently from behind my sofa, ate sparingly of tea (Inspector Home is very thin), and listened carefully at the door. When he heard Mrs. March approach, he insisted I open the door before she knocked. He gave her his "see-I-know-you're-coming" look and marched upstairs.

A few afternoons later, the merry friends gathered for tea and conversation. Helena, Lord Henry, Peter, and Shep were all there, and James, who was busy lurking, forgot to arrange the seating so that both Shep and Lord Henry were sitting on the sofa with Helena between them. James then placed himself between Helena and Shep, thereby preventing Shep from holding Helena's hand or patting her arm.

It was a happy time. We ate scones and strawberry jam and drank tea.

At last Peter said, "I have a request of Lord Henry. The album you brought me recently contains some letters that suggest there is a whole correspondence somewhere at Haverstock Hall. Would you search for it?"

Lord Henry looked both interested and distressed simultaneously.

"Dear Peter, of course I'll look, and enjoy doing so, but at present Etheria is staying at the Hall, and . . ." He didn't finish.

"I understand perfectly," said Peter. "It isn't so much that the correspondence would be valuable—though it would be—as that I suspect it would have historical interest. Just keep it in mind when you have time."

No more was said on the subject. Shep got up, asked Helena to go to dinner with him, and was turned down. Lord Henry was refused in his turn, and after hugging James, she left us. Shep went on his way and James, Lord Henry, and I at last went off to Frank's, where Lord Henry finally unburdened himself.

"I can't imagine what she wants!" he said, talking of Etheria. "She doesn't want me to marry. Says I'm too old. She wants me to give Haverstock Hall to the National Trust after we take everything we want to her castle in Scotland, but I don't know why. I've tried to talk to her frankly, but all she says is that she is concerned with my welfare and the honor of the family."

"I asked her, when she married Baggy, what she wanted from the old house, and she said she wouldn't think of taking anything that belonged to the house, but I suspect that was before I began thinking I'd like to marry Helena. Now she doesn't make any sense." Lord Henry sighed.

James had been listening carefully. He patted Lord Henry sharply on the arm.

Lord Henry looked up. "Yes, old chap?"

James gestured to himself.

"You?"

James nodded.

"You'd, ah, find out what Etheria wants?"

James nodded.

"How?" Lord Henry looked puzzled. James looked disgusted. He patted a catalog with a picture of Haverstock Hall on it that Lord Henry had put on the table.

"Take you to Haverstock Hall!" said Lord Henry happily. "Splendid! We'll all go down to look for the correspondence, Etheria or no Etheria."

James shook his head, pointed at me and shook his head again, then pointed at himself and nodded.

"Well," Lord Henry said, "Helena, then."

James shook his head firmly.

"Just you and me?"

James beamed. It took a while, but his dear friend had eventually caught on.

Two days later, arrangements had been made with Mrs. March, and Lord Henry arrived in his sports car on a glorious day. James snuggled down in the front seat and off they went.

In due time the sports car drove up the long driveway approaching Haverstock Hall. Before the car got to the entrance of the hall, James alerted Lord Henry to let him out, and—placing his paw on his mouth to indicate silence—disappeared into the shrubbery and slipped to the back of the hall, where he entered by the back door. Carefully keeping out of sight, he made his way to the door of the drawing room, waited till Wilson appeared with a tea cart, and slipped in when the door was opened. Wilson, occupied with maneuvering the tea cart, did not notice, and James slithered into invisibility behind the folds of a large blue silk drape from which he could see and hear but not be seen.

Waiting to dive into the lavish tea that Wilson was handing around were Etheria, the Marchioness, and Fiona. Lord Henry, looking fit and stocky, was standing before the large fireplace. He surveyed the women with some apprehension and strode out of the room, commenting, "Excuse me, I have work I must do. By the way, Wilson," he added, "set up a tea for me in the library, will you?"

"Very good, sir," said Wilson, and left.

"Do be careful what you do, dear," called Etheria to the retreating Lord Henry. "You are getting old and fragile, you know."

"Lord Henry certainly does look fragile," said Fiona, echoing Etheria as usual.

"Nonsense!" the Marchioness exclaimed. "He looks splendid, Ethy, almost blooming, you might say. Why do you insist he's over the hill?" She had just finished a smoked salmon and fresh dill sandwich, and now fell delightedly on an almond mocha cake.

"He's thinking of marrying again, and I know it would be terrible for him, all that turmoil and a new woman in the house," Etheria said mournfully.

"Imagine," said Fiona, "a new woman in the house."

The Marchioness laughed. "You don't want a new woman in the house!" she said. "You like it this way. You get the use of this house when you are tired of Baggy, and Henry doesn't interfere with you. If he married again, he'd live here most of the time, and his new wife would run the house."

"I'm not thinking of myself at all," said Etheria, much affronted. "I'm totally concerned with Henry's welfare. I'm proposing that he give the house to the National Trust."

"You are truly a saint," said Fiona, eating another mocha cake herself. "Henry will be dead in a week if he remarries."

"Well," said the Marchioness, "if you're really determined to give Haverstock Hall to the nation, will you give me your cook?" The Marchioness tried a strawberry tartlet this time.

"Oh, dear," said Etheria. "I should like nothing better, but I promised Mother dear on her deathbed that I should look after Cook, and I shall take her to Scotland and make sure she is comfortable for the rest of her life."

"You do honor all your responsibilities so!" said Fiona with a mouthful of apricot custard cake.

The Marchioness snorted and said, "You are something, Ethy!"

There was more gossip, and finally, having finished everything in sight, the three women at last left the room.

James had increased his store of information substantially. Etheria wanted Cook for her own house in Scotland, but what else? James was sure there was more on her mind.

He slithered out of the drawing room and padded noiselessly into the library, where he found Lord Henry napping on the big leather sofa before the fire. A glass of whiskey was on the coffee table, and the remains of a substantial tea were beside the whiskey. James sampled the whiskey and made inroads on the tea and had curled up at last next to his best friend when he heard the door open. He streaked under the sofa. Almost immediately he was nearly squashed flat as Etheria plumped down on the sofa. James could only listen.

"Henry," said Etheria, shaking him awake. "We must have a serious conversation. I have to make arrangements this week."

"What arrangements?" Lord Henry asked, pretending not to know.

"Why, packing all of our dear old things to go to

Scotland, of course! It's too much for you, this big house. You have your flat in London, and whenever you want country life surrounded by your own things, you have but to run up to us in Scotland at Reevers Roost—though I can't think why Baggy wants to call the castle by that terrible name—and Cook will give you all your favorite foods. . . ."

"Now, Ethy, this estate and the title and responsibilities are all mine, you understand. I inherited them when father died. At present, only you and I are involved. When I die, you inherit if I have no children. You have no children and are too old to have any, so there will be no future heirs from your side."

"I know," Etheria interrupted. "That is exactly why we should consolidate all of our assets in my place, and let the government take care of this estate."

"Etheria," Lord Henry said sternly, "Haverstock Hall and the title belong to me. When I die without issue, which it appears I will, you may do as you wish with this place if you are still alive, but until I die, I propose to make my own decisions for my own reasons."

"Are you planning to marry again?" Etheria asked.

"At the moment the only person I want to marry won't marry me," Lord Henry said sadly.

"Well," said Etheria, jumping up, "I'm glad someone has some sense. Not only are you too old, but it would be a desecration of Mathilda's memory. I am off to dress for dinner at the old Baron's. I've asked Wetherby to drive me. Now think over what I have said, and I'm sure you'll see that I'm right. If you don't see I'm right, I may have to take steps!" With that she flounced out of the library, and

144

James came out from underneath the couch. He sat on Lord Henry's lap and they both looked unhappy.

That evening, James slept in a dark corner of the hall. Etheria woke him when she came in from dinner and he followed her silently to her room, where he slipped in with her and hid.

Etheria sat at her dressing table and addressed her reflection in the mirror.

"Well," she said aloud, "I guess Henry will come around, but he had better hurry. I have only a month to find the ceremonial piece before the gala at the castle. It will be a spectacular asset to the party. There isn't a peer in Scotland or England who can match it. I'll see if Wilson can find it first thing in the morning, and if Henry objects I'll go to court." She smiled a self-satisfied smile at herself in the mirror, got up, put on her robe, and headed for the bathroom. James took the opportunity to slip out of the room.

The ceremonial piece! What on earth was that?

Before dawn, James hurried down to the kitchen to see if there were any leftovers, as he dared not let Cook or Wilson know he was in the house. He found three kippers on a plate and ate one. There was water in a plant bowl, which he drank, and thus refreshed, he waited concealed as Wilson appeared and shortly thereafter, as he suspected she would, Etheria arrived.

"Good morning, Madam," said Wilson, rising to his feet as she appeared.

"Wilson, I want to see the ceremonial piece!" She demanded.

"What?" said Wilson in surprise.

"You know," said Etheria impatiently. "That magnificent enameled silver and vermeil centerpiece that's been here for years."

Wilson looked puzzled. "I'm sorry, Lady Etheria, I haven't the slightest idea what you mean."

"Get the catalog." Etheria snapped.

Wilson went into the small office he had next to the kitchen, and returned with an old bound ledger book. Etheria snapped it out of his hands and riffled through pages in which were listed such things as "Staffordshire place setting for 24, Pantry 2, Cupboard 1," in various persons' handwriting. At last she found what she wanted, but she let out a gasp of anger.

"Here it is," she said. " 'Ceremonial centerpiece, silver, gold enamel, 11 pieces,' but no location. Wilson, why is there no location?"

"I truly don't know, Lady Etheria," said Wilson. "I've only been here seven years. I never heard of such a piece in all that time. Perhaps you should ask Lord Henry." Wilson was clearly very distressed.

Etheria banged the ledger closed, and slammed it on the kitchen table. "Thank you, Wilson," she said angrily, and stomped out.

Wilson picked up the ledger and returned it to his office, while James escaped from the kitchen to the library, where he sat in the knee hole of the desk to think.

Etheria wants Cook and the ceremonial piece. The ceremonial piece is somewhere in Haverstock Hall, but no one knows where. The next job for the great detective is to find the ceremonial piece. With this decision, James left his hiding place and, giving Lord Henry, who had just entered the library, a cheery salute, he slipped out into the great hall.

The rest of the day he spent in a systematic search. He explored every cupboard in all three pantries, and made a careful search of the many armoires and cabinets in the many unoccupied guest rooms, none of which were locked. This job was particularly arduous, as he had to pry the doors open and then push them shut again as silently as possible. Etheria had gone out, so he didn't have to be too careful, but there were the maids and Cook and Wilson to worry about.

In the storage room off the ballroom he found much dust and a lot of folding chairs.

In the children's nursery he found discarded toys and two big steamer trunks he could not open, but no ceremonial pieces.

Outside the nursery was a door that was slightly ajar. James slid inside and up a flight of dark, dusty stairs. He sneezed two or three times, raising more dust. He found himself in an attic illuminated only by the light from a tiny circular window. The attic was stacked with books, a broken chair was near the top of the stairs, and in the back was a cupboard barely visible in the dim light.

At first, James was tempted to give up. The attic was dirty, and no one had been here for years. He sat on a broken chair and sneezed again. At last he got off the chair, padded across the dusty floor, and entered the cupboard. It was totally dark, but James could feel something hard and bulky that seemed to be wrapped in a soft cloth. He found this object to be quite large, and as he was feeling around it, his paws slipped on something small, also in some sort of cloth.

147

Fastidiously he took the small object in his mouth and hopped out of the cupboard with it. In the dim light he saw he had a gray flannel bag, tied up with a silk cord, which contained something hard and lumpy. Holding the cord in his mouth, he carried the bag bouncing down the attic stairs. He dragged it along the hall, intending to take it to the library to show Lord Henry, when a voice on the stairs called out, "Make yourself comfortable in the drawing room, Fiona!"

Etheria was hurrying upstairs. James dropped the silken cord and hid behind a chest of drawers.

Etheria did not see James, but she did see the sack. For a moment she stopped, then swooped down, picked up the sack, and hurried off to her own room.

James went to the drawing room and concealed himself behind the window draperies to await developments.

Fiona sat looking out the window while Wilson wheeled in a tea cart. Lord Henry poked his head in the door and instructed Wilson to leave him a big tea in the library and not clear up until the morning. Then he left. Etheria entered with the flannel bag in her hand. She was clearly excited.

"Fiona!" she cried. "I've found it!"

And she opened the little bag and produced what appeared to be a sort of small bowl held up by a nude girl sitting on a mound of thistles, all in silver. The inside of the bowl was gilded, and the leaves and flowers of the this-tles were enameled green and purple.

"What on earth is that!" Fiona exclaimed.

"The ceremonial piece!" Etheria cried. "I found it on the stairs. I wonder how it got there. Fiona, it means the whole thing is still here. It is truly glorious when it is assembled."

At last Etheria put the dish down on a footstool in front of the hearth, on which a fire was burning brightly. The dish glittered.

Fiona's hands also held an object, a small gold bell in the shape of an Elizabethan woman whose head and shoulders were the bell's handle, and whose skirt spread out to form the bell. In the woman's hand was clasped a large ruby. Fiona looked with envy at both objects, and then placed the bell on the footstool beside the enameled dish.

Etheria poured tea and babbled away about how wonderful all the treasures of Haverstock Hall would be in her own great castle, particularly the ceremonial piece.

Fiona sighed and said nothing.

At last, tea all gone, the two women left, Etheria to change for dinner at the Marchioness's. Neither woman thought to take the two objects on the footstool.

The room was warm and quiet, and James dozed. Then he was rudely awakened by a scratching sound.

Instantly alert, James watched the firelight glinting on the precious metal. The scratching continued. From underneath the skirt of a small side chair against the wall next to the fireplace, a furry gray form appeared. Two black, beady eyes looked furtively around. Then their owner, a rat, scurried up to the footstool, scrambled up on it, picked up the bell, and scurried back under the chair. James was fascinated. The process was repeated, but this time the rat carried off the little dish.

James considered. He left his hiding place under the drapes and began to shove against the chair. It was light and moved easily. Behind it, James found a sizable hole in the molding at floor level. He examined the paneling carefully, and then, satisfied with what he saw, jumped on the chair, and from there to the stone mantelpiece, and crouching on the ledge of the mantel, he examined the carving of flowers and leaves that supported the mantel ledge. After only a brief examination, he hit one of the flowers sharply with his paw. There was a creaking sound, and a section of the paneling next to the fireplace opened about a foot.

James jumped down and entered the opening. From the firelight in the room, he could see he was in a space large enough for a man to hide in. In one corner of this space was a rat's nest. The rat had disappeared at the sound of the panel's opening. In the nest were a number of objects. The bell, the dish, a pair of diamond earrings, and three teaspoons.

James touched nothing, but smiled to himself and returned to the drawing room, jumped up on the mantel, and patted the flower, causing the panel to close. Then he slipped out of the drawing room and stopped by the library, where he found the delicious remains of a tea that offered sardines, liver sausage, and Laphroaig, all apparently left over from Lord Henry's tea, but really arranged for James. After tea, James curled up under the desk for the night.

Next morning he was up with the dawn and sitting in the drawing room. Lying on the hearth was a sardine that he had carefully saved from tea the day before. As expected, the rat appeared shortly, lured by the sardine. Swiftly and surely, James struck, and a dead rat lay at his feet. James, who doesn't relish rat, laid its body beside the chair, where it was safely hidden. In no time he had opened the panel, brought out the bell, dish, earrings, and three spoons, and arranged them next to the rat. Then he closed the panel again, and pushed the little chair over the display. No sooner was he finished than he heard a noise in the hall and hid behind the drapes.

Etheria entered the drawing room in a rage. She looked on the footstool, then all over the room, on the tops of tables and in the sofa. She could not find what she wanted and stormed out in a rage, not bothering to close the door behind her.

Sounds of turmoil could be heard throughout the house. The uproar grew fainter as she made her way to the kitchen, and James was about to explore further when Lord Henry and Helena appeared. They stood very close together, looking out the very window where James was concealed in the drapery.

"I had to come," she said. "I have changed my mind. As you know, I've been spending a lot of time by myself lately, trying to solve our problems. I find there is only one solution. I love you and I will marry you, and if Etheria makes a fuss, we will have to live through it. I care about you, and if she wants Haverstock Hall and all the things in it, let her have it all."

She said this all in a rush, and then stood looking vulnerable.

Lord Henry beamed and grabbed her around her waist, and she bent her head to receive his resounding kiss. Then they wandered hand in hand around the room until the uproar returned to the drawing room with Etheria in the lead and Wilson and an underfootman in tow. The underfootman looked very angry, and Wilson did not look happy.

"Henry," Etheria cried, pointing at the footman, "this man is a thief. I want him arrested immediately." She stopped to notice Helena.

"Wait in the hall," she commanded. "We have a domestic crisis here."

Lord Henry looked sternly at his sister.

"Etheria, sit down!" he said firmly. He installed Helena in a chair across the room and stood on the hearth. It gave him a little height.

"Now, Wilson, what does this seem to be about?" he asked.

Etheria leaped from her chair. "Sit down, Etheria, you can have your say as soon as I have heard from Wilson."

Etheria, nonplussed by Lord Henry's firmness, sat.

"Lady Etheria reported to me this morning that the bell was missing, as well as a part of something called the ceremonial piece," Wilson replied. "I note that the bell is not in its usual place, so it may be missing. I have to report that three teaspoons from our commonly used set are also missing. They are not valuable, but the bell, of course, is. Very."

"It certainly is priceless," said Etheria, jumping up, "and this footman was out last evening, hiding it somewhere."

"I didn't take anything!" said the footman, who was very angry. "I don't know what her ladyship is talking about."

"Well," Etheria said, shifting her ground. "Perhaps *she* took it. How do we know how long she's been hanging around!" and she looked directly at Helena.

Lord Henry was now very angry.

"Etheria," he said, "apologize to the future Lady Haverstock immediately. You must be out of your head to make such an accusation. If need be, I shall call Inspector Home of Scotland Yard to investigate, and you shall return to Scotland immediately he does not need you. This is my home, and I will conduct its affairs as I see fit."

"You are incompetent!" Etheria shouted. "You have no sense of possession. You've let the ceremonial piece get away, and now the Elizabethan bell is gone. I'll sue."

Since all the parties to this wrangle were occupied with their own anger, none of them noticed when a side chair began to move, revealing a tableau that included a dead rat, a pair of diamond earrings, three spoons, a gold and ruby bell, and a vermeil salt dish.

James then trotted over to Lord Henry and patted his leg.

"James!" cried Helena in delight.

"Gaaack . . . ugh," gargled Etheria.

Lord Henry looked down inquiringly.

James pointed to the tableau on the floor. Helena, who had jumped up when she saw James, knelt down at the display.

"A rat!" she exclaimed. "There is your culprit. Wilson, here are your spoons, and Etheria, your bell." Helena handed out the objects. "Here is a pair of diamond earrings. They look very valuable to me. I wonder who owns them?"

Etheria grabbed them. Her face was very flushed. "They're mine," she said in a strangled voice. "I must have left them here on that footstool at Christmas. They hurt, you know."

153

"I remember," Lord Henry said firmly. "You accused your maid of stealing them."

"Good riddance, she left the next week anyway!" said Etheria.

"And what is this strange dish?" Helena asked, holding the object in her hands.

"It is one of the pieces of the ceremonial centerpiece," said Etheria. "I found it on the stairs where I thought this fellow had dropped it." She glared at the footman.

Lord Henry ignored Etheria and turned to the footman. "My sincere apologies, Jensen." He said. "Regardless of the statements of my sister, I did not think for a minute that you had stolen anything. I am only deeply sorry that you have been subjected to this ugly scene."

Jensen smiled and nodded.

"Wilson," Lord Henry continued, "let's clear up this rat. I wonder where it came from, anyway?"

James hopped to the chair, and from there to the mantel, where he patted the flower to open the panel.

"The priest hole!" Lord Henry exclaimed. "I'd been told about it, but I had no idea where it was. James, you are clever."

Lord Henry instructed Wilson to clean out the rat's nest and have the molding repaired, and was about to go off with Helena to the stables for a ride, when James let out a sharp cough.

"Yes, James?" Said Lord Henry.

James beckoned to the group and headed up the stairs. Of course, they all followed. Lord Henry and Helena led the way; Etheria, dying of curiosity, followed, even though she could not bear to be near "that cat." Wilson and Jensen brought up the rear.

Up the stairs, down the hall, past the nursery to the attic door, and up the attic stairs they went.

"Wilson, some flashlights," called Lord Henry.

In a very short time the group was crowded into the attic, now illuminated with flashlights, and out of the cupboard at the back came object after object, wrapped in gray flannel bags.

Now the troupe returned to the dining room in reverse, Wilson and Jensen in the lead with some large objects, and Etheria, Helena, and Lord Henry with small ones.

Once in the great dining hall, chairs were moved away from the table so that Wilson and Jensen could work. Wrappings were removed, and at last the ceremonial piece was revealed in all its grandeur.

In the center of the table was an allegorical group consisting of a Scottish warrior and an English warrior standing side by side. Immediately behind and above them, a bosomy woman in flowing draperies held a laurel wreath over the head of each warrior. Between them was a shield inscribed with the words "Made for Etheria, Lady Haverstock, William Revere, 1720." Backing up the warriors and facing in the opposite direction were four young girls draped with garlands of thistles and roses and little else, labeled "Courage," "Valor," "Truth," and "Honor." The whole of this company stood on what appeared to be some craggy rocks on a base engirdled with garlands of thistles and roses.

This astonishing piece stood about three feet high and was nearly six feet long. The bottom was heavily felted. It was made of silver, and the uniforms of the warriors were rendered in blazing enameled colors that were particularly effective on the plaid of the Scotsman. The roses were pink and the thistles purple, with green leaves all around. Here and there were touches of gilding.

In addition to the centerpiece there were two large candelabra, each of which could hold five candles. One was a rose tree, and the other, of course, was a giant thistle.

In addition to all this splendor, there were twelve salt dishes, six with beautiful maidens and six with youthful males. There was also a large leather box with place-card holders and other supplementary pieces of table gear, all in the same exuberant spirit.

Etheria clasped her hands and sighed. "Isn't it wonderful!" she breathed. "It is absolutely glorious, England and Scotland wedded forever!"

Lord Henry was overcome with a fit of coughing, and Helena, apparently overcome with emotion, stood looking out the dining room windows, her shoulders shaking. James hopped on the table and tapped a salt dish, which rolled along happily on its ball bearings.

Lord Henry said a few whispered words to Helena, and she nodded her head. Then he turned to his sister.

"Etheria," he said, "would you like to have this arrangement as a wedding present?"

"Are you serious?" Etheria asked, unable to credit her hearing. "Would you give it up?"

"Helena and I think it belongs at Reever's Roost with you and Baggy. Take it as a wedding present, with our blessing."

"Please," said Helena who had recovered her composure. "I feel it belongs with the eldest Haverstock, and just because you happen to be a woman is no reason you should be deprived of something you clearly love. We can come and see it any time we want."

"I'm sure that is very gracious of you," Etheria said ungraciously. She turned to Wilson. "Pack it carefully, and I'll take it tomorrow." Then she turned back to Lord Henry and said, "I guess if you are going to marry her, you will be staying on here after all."

"Yes. I think we will," said Lord Henry.

"Will you want Cook?" Etheria asked, ever hopeful.

Helena started to say something, and Lord Henry stopped her.

James looked up apprehensively.

"We will want Cook," Lord Henry said firmly. James let out a sigh of relief, and Wilson smiled a broad smile.

"Very well." said Etheria. "I'll go and pack, and perhaps Weatherby can drive me home in the station wagon with the piece."

"Certainly," said Lord Henry.

And so, that afternoon, Etheria went off to tea at the Marchioness's place after arranging to return to Reever's Roost the next day with her earrings and the ceremonial piece.

Helena, Lord Henry, and James sat in the library in front of the fire, ate Cook's best tea, and giggled the afternoon away.

At last James, his detective assignment complete, fell asleep exhausted, and Lord Henry and Helena went happily about their own business.

CHAPTER 11

It was time to return to London. Jensen, trying desper-
ately to suppress a grin, loaded the station wagon. Wilson,
his eyes twinkling, supervised. James jumped into the car,
and finally Helena and Lord Henry came out hand in
hand.

"Good-bye for now, Lady Haverstock," said Wilson.

"Still Helena Haakon," Helena laughed. "But not for
long."

Weatherby, whistling happily, drove to London,
where James was deposited at Baron's Chambers, Helena
at her flat, and Lord Henry at his club.

For the next weeks, life took on a special excitement.
A wedding was coming up. The band of friends met often
in my flat for conferences and cups of tea or drams of whiskey, whichever was preferred. During the day, James went
about his usual business at Baron's or Thwaite's.

One afternoon, Peter Hightower dropped in for a wee
drop and reported on some old business. It seems that Mr.
Poachway, whose real name was Mohammed Rafik Nasser,
was still operating the Temple of Bastet. He had replaced
James with a photo mural of a big gray cat, and during
services from time to time he told the story of the manifes-
tation of Bastet that came, uninvited, to bless this particular temple with his/her presence for a brief time. Those

communicants who had actually seen James at the temple could, and often did, corroborate the truth of this assertion. So the temple prospered and James the God was not forgotten.

Inspector Home sent his regards through a note to Peter but actually meant for James. It recounted the fate of the stamp thief, who had been sent to prison along with his confederate, a maid in the collector's household. The collector had been shaken by the events, and now kept his collection in safety deposit boxes in a bank.

"Your influence has spread far and wide," said Peter, stroking James, who was sitting on his lap with his eyes closed.

"Now bring me up to date on the wedding of the century," said Peter, turning to Helena.

"Well, complications have arisen," Helena said. "We are not only going to have a wedding, but a midsummer celebration, church fête, and village fair, all at the same time."

"Bloody Bruce!" exclaimed Baggy, who, in his capacity as best man, often dropped in of an afternoon. "How did you get into all that?"

"We set the date for Sunday, June twenty-fourth," said Helena. "The vicar agreed. We planned a simple four-o'clock wedding with a reception to follow at the hall, and then Fiona called me to say that the Women's Exchange had planned a summer festival to raise money, and at the same time to help revive old customs. The only weekend possible was that of the twenty-third."

"Henry and I agreed that there should be no conflict, as the wedding would not be until Sunday and the church

159

would not be required for the fête, competition, and cultural program, all of which would take place on the village common."

"I would gladly have changed the date, except that the invitations were all engraved. However, it seems there was more to it than just a slight conflict. Fiona wanted Henry and me to appear, sit on a dais, give out the prizes, and watch the Morris and maypole dancers. She said it would add a marvelous note to the proceedings."

"I was ready to say no," said Lord Henry, "but then, when I saw how sad Fiona looked at the prospect, and I thought how mad it would make Etheria to think of our associating ourselves with local village life, and when Helena said she thought it would be fun—I changed my mind and agreed."

"I think it should be a treat," said Peter. "Some of the wedding guests will be there to add their huzzahs to those of the local residents, not to mention their money to the coffers of the sale. Besides, I haven't seen Morris dancing in years."

James opened his eyes and tapped Peter on the arm in a fidgety way.

"What's Morris dancing?" Baggy asked.

James nodded as if to reinforce Baggy's question.

"Well," said Peter, font of all knowledge, "as I understand it, Morris dancing was brought from Spain, some say by John of Gaunt. It involved some five or six men and originally a boy dressed as a girl. On their legs the men wore bells that were tuned to add to the music, and later some elements of the Robin Hood story were added, so that the girl became Maid Marian and the leader of the dancers became Robin Hood. The whole thing was abolished with the arrival of Cromwell and the Puritans. However, there seems to be some sort of revival going on."

"That seems to be what it is all about," said Lord Henry. "In addition, Fiona, who isn't too accurate historically about all this, wants to have a maypole dance to climax the proceedings."

"I think it will be splendid, and add to the festivity of the day," said Helena, smiling. "Of course, if it rains, the whole thing will be postponed for a week. Not the wedding, of course—just the fête, the fair, and the cultural event."

That evening, Lord Henry and Helena went off for dinner together. Peter, James, and I went to Frank's for dinner, and after a substantial meal of linguine and clam sauce, James practiced his idea of Morris dance steps on the table.

Peter and I were in a reminiscent mood, particularly because I would have to leave London right after the wedding. My assignments for the year were finished.

So we sat over our coffee and talked of all the events of the past few months until James could no longer think of new dance steps and insisted we go home.

The days flew by. Almost everyone accepted the wedding invitation. Wedding presents poured in at Haverstock Hall, where they were set out on a big table in the morning room. Helena's maid of honor, a delightful redheaded girl named Poppy Balsom, agreed to take over the lease on Helena's apartment. Mrs. March agreed that James could go to the wedding, and even go a day or two early, since Helena and Lord Henry particularly wanted him.

And so it was that Weatherby drove James and me to Haverstock Hall early in the week of the wedding.

The hall had been transformed. Even in the short few weeks since she had agreed to become Lady Haverstock, Helena had made important changes. The gold and white furniture in the big drawing room had been replaced with comfortable sofas and chairs, and it was now an inviting place to visit. Throughout the house, heavy velvet draperies had been eliminated. Light poured into the rooms, and precious furniture that could be damaged by sunlight had been stored, or given to the National Trust.

Wilson and his staff were preparing for the reception, which was to include a huge buffet and dancing as well as drinks.

James toured the house, a job he considered his duty as the best friend of the lord of the manor. However, the brilliant sunlight outside beckoned, and James decided to explore the activities on the village common.

On the common, an acre of grass in the center of the village, groups of men, women, boys, and girls were deep in physical activity. Morris dancers with bells on their feet were stamping and kicking in one corner. A group of boys were practicing hitting a target with a lance while riding on the shoulders of bigger boys. Tumblers were going through their routines. In fact, the common was filled with activity. There was very little conversation to be heard. The air was largely filled with grunts, interspersed with an occasional "Watch it!" or "That's sloppy work." James stretched first his front legs, then his hind ones, and prepared to enter athletics. Of course, he assured himself, he could do anything athletic better than anyone else. The fact

162

that physical effort took training, and that by and large he was a sedentary cat, given to drinking single-malt whiskey and eating Fortnum & Mason's crab salad did not enter his head.

He joined the Morris dancers and learned their routine easily, but he tired quickly. On his way to the tumblers he passed a maypole that had been set up temporarily in the center of the common.

A maypole did not usually stand in the center of the common. In fact, there had not been one for fifteen years, and this one would come down right after the fête; the hole that had been dug to hold the pole would be filled in immediately, and although it wasn't properly anchored, it would do for the dance.

James stood at the bottom and looked up. The maypole was some fifteen feet high and looked, from James's vantage point, as though it reached the sky.

"Hey, cat," said a passing dancer, "don't climb that pole, you'll never get down again."

"Scat," hissed a companion dancer to James, then asked the first dancer, "Why are you talking to that cat? He can't understand you."

"Dunno," said the first. "Just seemed the thing to do." They stamped off, jingling the bells around their ankles.

James appraised the pole thoughtfully, and then joined the tumblers. He found he was very good at somersaults, and that he could walk a balance beam on four legs but not, to his distress, on two. He tried to do a backward somersault, but failed. He tried leaping into the air and executing a twist, but failed utterly. His only successes were his landings. Always on his feet.

There was more to this athletic business than he had thought. He eyed the pole again.

Weary from all the activity, he collapsed next to a bench where a pair of elderly women were talking and observing the scene.

"Last time we had a maypole, some dumb cat climbed it and the fire department had to get it down," said one.

"I wonder what's so hard about it," said the other. "Cats can climb trees both up and down."

"Well, I hope one doesn't try it this time," said the other.

James looked back at the pole. So no cat had successfully climbed up and down that pole. He would show them a thing or two!

As the afternoon wore on, the athletes departed for the day and James was left alone. He approached the pole and placed a tentative paw on its smooth side. He started climbing up. It was harder than he had thought it would be, but he persevered. Finally, muscles tired, he reached the top. What a glorious sight! He could see the green where a platform had been set up with its back to the road. On this platform the dignitaries would sit for the dances and maypole event. Beyond the platform was the road, and across the road was a row of shops well known to James because he had visited most of them at Christmas. The road was nearly empty, but he noticed in front of the jeweler's shop a girl who looked vaguely familiar, accompanied by a young man. The girl was looking in the window of the shop with great intensity. The man was looking around furtively.

On the opposite side of the common was a small

woods. The road split at the corner past the shops, and houses lined the side that bounded the green. The other side of the common was bounded by the churchyard.

James surveyed all sides of the common, puzzled for a moment over the problem of where he had seen the girl before, and then tackled the problem of how to get down.

After all the comments he had heard, he felt he had to get down himself, there were no two ways about that. He tried going down headfirst; that was impossible. At last, infinitely slowly, taking time with each move, he climbed down backward and returned to Haverstock Hall, where he wolfed down a huge meal in the kitchen and curled up on my bed. He was exhausted but happy. *I did it,* he thought. *But who is that girl?* Then he fell asleep.

During the night it rained, but in the morning the day sparkled, and all morning the sales booths set up along the side of the green bounded by the churchyard were busy. A lunch tent had been set up on the side of the green facing the houses, and the road had been blocked there for the day so that those serving the lunches could get back and forth easily to the houses where supplies were kept. In the afternoon, various contests took place in the center of the common around the maypole.

During the afternoon, Lord Henry, Helena, and all the members of the wedding party who wanted to participate, as well as village dignitaries and, of course, James, sat on the platform. The shops across the street had done a good business during the day, what with people coming and going all the time. As the contests began, the sales staffs of the shops came across the road to stand on the edge of the common and watch.

Prizes were awarded, and beaming villagers took home ribbons for best delphinium and biggest beetroot. The winners of the athletic contest received small cups. At last the cultural part of the program began and the Morris dancers, their bells tuned to an uncertain harmony, stamped around the common. As they disappeared, a certain confusion ensued as the grammar school children gathered for madrigal singing. Under cover of this activity, James slipped off the platform and headed for the maypole, which was now draped with pink and white ribbons attached to a disc on the top. As he started to climb, his progress was hidden by the ribbons. No one paid any attention. He navigated over the edge of the disc and sat on its middle atop the pole and surveyed the scene, grinning with self-satisfaction.

The sun moved in the heavens, songs and skits were over, and James was almost sleepy.

As the maypole dancers picked up their ribbons he was jerked sharply awake.

The maypole dance was the closing event of the day, and a goodly crowd surrounded the common. Most of the merchants had left their shops and come across the street to see the finale. The village constable rested his bicycle against the platform and stood on it to watch.

Some ten boys and an equal number of girls dressed in white circled the maypole, weaving the ribbons into a mesh pattern against the pole and gradually getting closer and closer to it.

The pole had been slightly loosened by the rain during the night. The ground under it was soft, and the press of young people around it, pulling first in one direction, then

166

another, widened the top of the hole in which the pole was placed.

The once confident James began to feel just slightly seasick as the top of the pole began to make a small circle through the air. The more the dancers danced, the wider grew the circle the top of the pole made, and the sicker James got. He began to look around frantically. Suddenly he noticed—across the street at the jewelry store—the girl, the girl he had seen months ago at Baron's Chambers, who had left so precipitously. She was looking in the jewelry store window, and the man with her was trying to break open the door.

James, frightened by the now widely swinging pole and concerned about a possible robbery, let out a wild howl at the top of his not inconsiderable voice. At the same time he lifted a paw and pointed in the direction of the shop.

The dancers froze. The spectators looked first at James, and then, as he waved his paw, they turned around and looked across the street. The constable jumped down and raced to the jewelry shop, where he collared the man, who was also frozen by the howls that continued from the top of the maypole.

The dance had stopped. The pole sagged to one side. James sat shaking on the tilted disc. Helena, ever resourceful, had left the platform where confusion reigned as people tried to sort out what was happening where. She got some of the boys to remove a canvas awning from one of the booths, and then boys and girls together held the edges of the awning under the spot where James was sitting, sick and frightened.

"James," Helena called when all was ready, "you've saved us from great trouble, and now we'll save you."

"Jump," she cried. "We'll catch you."

But James had made his own decision, and so, laboriously, sometimes headfirst and sometimes the other way round, he climbed down the tilted pole. There was resounding applause as his paw touched the ground. He walked with great dignity the three steps necessary to reach Helena's arms, and then collapsed.

The maypole was righted. The music began again, and the dancers once again wound and unwound their pink and white ribbons. Only the village constable and two would-be thieves did not see it.

The next afternoon, Helena and Lord Henry were married in a lovely ceremony. James sat next to me in one of the front pews. He was stiff but content.

There was a splendid reception. Everyone assured Fiona that the fête, sale, and cultural event had been a huge success. Footmen passed champagne, and the buffet was laid out in the dining room. There was dancing in the drawing room, and games were played in the billiard room. The party lasted well into the early hours.

James recovered rapidly and frolicked about, lapping champagne and eating lobster until he wore himself out and curled up on my bed.

We were both up fairly early the next morning, and James limped down to a great English breakfast. Afterwards, we said good-bye to Lord Henry and Lady Helena, who hugged us both, and then we were driven back to Baron's by Weatherby.

I now packed again, while James supervised, because

168

I was leaving Baron's for the year. My work was finished, at least for the present.

As I finished packing, I said to James, "We ought to have something really special tonight."

James nodded.

I got out the carrying bag. It needed dusting, for James had not needed to use it for some time. He hopped in, and we headed for Fortnum & Mason.

There I was again, with a cat in a bag, peering at the delicacies in the cases.

"Shall we have some caviar?" I asked the air.

The bag mewed.

"A jar of your best beluga caviar," I told the clerk. We added some melba toast and some Devonshire cream because James loves Devonshire cream on absolutely anything, and a bottle of Old Bushmills single-malt for a change, and I hurried back to my flat with a parcel in one hand and a cat in a bag in the other.

And so, at last, sated with delicious things to eat and drink, I was prepared to sit and watch the late news with my eyes closed in company with my friend. But James had other ideas. He rose and waved me to the door. In passing, he picked up the carrying bag in this teeth and dragged it with him. I opened the door to the flat. James deposited the bag outside the door, then returned, and we watched the news together after all.

At eleven-thirty there was a knock at the door.

There, as usual, was Mrs. March. "Is James here?" she asked.

Also, as usual, James was on the stairs behind her, this time sitting on the carrying bag. He waved a paw and headed upstairs, dragging the bag with him.

Next morning when the cab arrived, there was James, sitting on his table, ready to look over a new tenant. A rare personality indeed!